RELEVANT NOVELS BY HARRY KATZAN, JR.
A Matt and the General Series

Life is Good
Everything is Good
The Last Adventure
The Romeo Affair
Another Romeo Affair
Understanding

USEFUL BOOKS BY HARRY KATZAN, JR.

Service and Advanced Technology
Everything is Good
A Collection of Service Essays
The Little Book of Artificial Intelligence
A Tale of Discovery
The Little Book of Cybersecurity

Lessons in Artificial Intelligence

WITH MATT, ASHLEY AND THE GENERAL

Harry Katzan Jr.

LESSONS IN ARTIFICIAL INTELLIGENCE
WITH MATT, ASHLEY AND THE GENERAL

iUniverse books may be ordered through booksellers or by contacting:

iUniverse
1663 Liberty Drive
Bloomington, IN 47403
www.iuniverse.com
844-349-9409

ISBN: 978-1-6632-5494-8 (sc)
ISBN: 978-1-6632-5495-5 (hc)
ISBN: 978-1-6632-5496-2 (e)

Library of Congress Control Number: 2023913765

Print information available on the last page.

iUniverse rev. date: 07/24/2023

For Margaret, with all my love
now and forever

Main Characters in the Book

The General – Les Miller. Former military General and Humanitarian. P-51 pilot and World War II hero.

Matthew (Matt) Miller – Professor of Mathematics. Grandson of the General. Sophisticated problem solver and strategist.

Ashley Wilson Miller – College friend of Matt Miller. Former Duchess of Bordeaux. Married to Matt Miller. Is a Receiver of the National Medal of Freedom.

General Clark - Mark Clark. Former Four Star General and Chairman of the Joint Chiefs of Staff. Appointed to be U.S. Director of Intelligence.

Kimberly Scott – The Intelligence specialist of the U.S.

Katherine Penelope Radford – Retired Queen of the United Kingdom and personal friend of the General.

END OF CHARACTERS

Introduction

This is a novel about Artificial Intelligence. As unusual as it sounds, there is a very good reason for its existence. There are existing books on the subject that are very good but are very difficult to read. It's that simple. The concepts are complicated and some require complex math.

Artificial Intelligence is here to stay this time. It's a third try to bring then the subject to the forefront. It is here for the future, and it is here to stay because the world needs it. We are in the midst of war, preparation for defense, a dismal economic outlook, crime, killing, and so forth. We need it because if we continue the way we are going, we won't be going anywhere for very long. Practically everything is disarray. Just name them: violence, shady politics, global warming, discrimination, abortion, women's birth problems, men's cancer. What is the solution? It is twofold. Equitably use the information we have and permit the human race to communicate and act in a reasonable manner. Through Artificial Intelligence, often referred to as AI, we have the key to managing our lives on a daily basis – worldwide.

Instead of business and government leaders having to tell us what they are going to do, we can and will be addressing that subject through AI.

AI is a systems concept, not a single piece of software you can buy at a local store. Can you imagine a kid telling you they have computers and AI, meaning software apps.

So, here is what we are providing to you with in this book. A straightforward description of the subject of AI embedded in an easy-to-read novel. Even if you don't like AI, you will love the novel. The major characters are Matt Miller, who has a PhD from a prestigious university, his wife Ashley, also a professor, who is a dramatic woman with an ingenious mind, and General Les Miller, Matt's grandfather, who is a former a war-hero pilot and the founder of a very profitable business. Matt uses his mathematical thinking to solve complex problem, with the assistance of Ashley, and the leadership of the General.

The book is not expensive and something you would enjoy giving to a relative or friend. The book adheres to the author's principle of no sex, no violence, and no bad language. It is accessible to all readers.

Enjoy it if you can,
The Author

PS: The book contains an AI index and an AI report at the tail end. Now you can really enjoy it.

Contents

Part IV
The Team Gets Down to Business

Part V
The Final Result

PART I

Cleaning Things Up and Introducing the Characters

(CHAPTERS 1 THROUGH 4)

CHAPTER 1

Life Without the General

It was a cool and breezy morning and the bedroom window had been open all night. Ashley rolled over and looked at the clock. It was 6 o'clock, and Matt was asleep. She cozied over next to him and tried to awaken him. He was dead to the world, but a couple of nudges did the job.

"Are you okay?" asked Matt. "I know, you expected to hear the phone ring."

"It is strange, I did," said Ashley. "I complained like the dickens, and now I miss it. I wonder how the General is doing with the former Queen and what he does all day."

"I wonder if they are treating him nicely," replied Matt. "The British media are well known for giving a newcomer a rough time. Living in England and residing with the royalty must be a tremendous challenge. He can't just go out and take a walk. He can't go to Starbucks for a grande coffee. I wonder if he is playing any golf, and with whom."

"Who washes his clothes," said Ashley. "Does he brush his own teeth. I think they bring the teeth washing facility right to him."

"I wonder what kind of car he gets to drive, and where he gets to go if he has one," continued Matt. "Maybe he gets driven around, if he gets to go anywhere."

"I wonder what he gets to eat, and what is his choice of coffee, tea, milk, or water," said Ashley. "Does he get to watch the telly or get to read books."

"Do they sleep in the same room?" asked Matt. "I've heard that royalty do not, and I wonder why. What does he do in the evening, and what time does retire for the night? Does she ever get angry with him? Does he get the beef he likes so much, and does he drink his scotch, like he used to. What does she call him and he call her? Does he have a cell phone and what happened to his satellite phone. Is the palace warm or cold? What kind of clothes does he wear during the day? I wonder if he would like to come home."

"How can we find the answers to those questions and others that we haven't thought of?" said Ashley. "Does he ever think of us? Does he ever see or talk to his buddy Buzz.? What kind of shoes does he wear in the palace? How are the bathing facilities and the loo? I wonder what the loo paper is like. I wonder if he has even been out of the palace yet."

"I think we should call Buzz." Said Matt. "He might be wondering the same things that we are. In this country, the General was always the boss, speaking casually. There, he is not anybody. It seems like the retired Queen is a fussy eater. The

General is a robust eater. I'll get us some coffee and then I will call Buzz. It's the middle of the day there."

"No, you talk to Buzz, and I'll get the coffee," replied Ashley. "Do you know where your satellite phone is? I'll get it."

"It's on my desk," said Matt. "And, bring me some paper and a pen. No. Bring one of those notebooks. This might end up being a big deal."

Matt sat on the edge of the bed with his nightstand on his right. He put on his slippers, and then gave himself a little belly laugh. Put on your slippers to talk to someone on a phone. Ashley returned in 6 minutes with two cups of Keurig coffee on a tray, a notebook and pen in her left hand, and the satellite phone in her pocket. Ashley liked to do things for people.

Matt dialed Buzz on his satellite phone, and Buzz answered on the first ring.

"Sir Charles here," said Buzz, whose real name is Charles Bunday, Knight of the Royal Kingdom, and former Army buddy of the General."

"Hi Buzz," said Matt, "This is Matt in the States."

"Matt, it's good to hear from you," replied Buzz. "I was wondering how you and Ashley were doing without the General."

"We're okay," said Matt, "It's the General that we are concerned about. What have you heard?"

"Well, I have a bombshell," said Buzz. "The London media is all over the General and so is our friend Katherine Penelope Radford. It seems your general is an independent sole and she doesn't like it. She is talking to the media and she is laying it on thick. It seems that he didn't like the first dinner and he said in a loud voice that he wanted real food and not this female junk. He stormed out, called a car, which the retired Queen didn't like, and headed for the closest pub and, as the media wrote, 'ate them out of business'. The men in London love him. He's their hero, and the women call him their American, and who knows what else."

"Even the King liked him," said Buzz, "and the American, as they call him, is the best thing that ever happened to the kingdom. The entire country is in an joyous uproar."

"He demanded a sporty BMW to get to the golf course and wouldn't let the royal staff even touch his new set of American clubs," continued Buzz. "The country cancelled a polo match to watch him play golf. He has a tail of followers behind him day and night. They call him the retired Queen's real man. He's got all the men and the younger women on his side. At first it was the younger female group up to about 40 years old, and now it's up to 60. There isn't a golf club in the country to be purchased; they are all sold out. I would say the country sport is now golf, and even the women are now playing golf, and so am I."

"Well, I'll be," said Matt.

"You have got to get him out of here, Matt," said Buzz. "They will be calling the United Kingdom the colony of America. Travel from England to the United States has increased 100 fold, and the English resorts are having to close up. People are buying American clothes and using American English. Little kids are walking around saying, "I am an American" and no one seems to mind."

"I'll take care of it," said Matt. "Ashley and I will come over in the Gulfstream and do it, but we have to make a plan. We've done it before. Please get us landing rights or whatever to the London City Airport. I'll be flying unless I can round up those two retired F-22 Raptor pilots. Try to get ahold of the General and let him know that Ashley and I will take care of it."

"One more thing," said Buzz. "I'm am now a national hero, since the General and I were former Army buddies. I have to be a little careful what I do. So I have some limitations when making your plan. Maybe we should use the Military Air Base just north of London."

"I'll call you in two hours," said Matt.

END OF CHAPTER ONE

CHAPTER 2

The Plan to Save Their General

"Well, it's very interesting," said Matt.

"I heard every word of it," said Ashley. "For some reason it made me proud to be an American and happy to know the General. I guess we more than know him. We've experienced him, and I say that is the best sense."

"We need to make a plan to extract him, as we've done before, and we could use that little notebook you have in your hand," said Matt.

"Do you think the method we used before would be suitable or should we develop a more classy plan?" asked Ashley. "Having the extracted person drown would work, but it is not up to the sophistication and stature of the General. He would wish he had drowned if we did it that way."

"That's a good point," answered Matt. "Let's go to Starbucks. We seem to think better there. We only have 2 hours so bring your pad."

Both Matt and Ashley had a blueberry scone and a grande coffee. They sat by the window so only one side of them was visible.

"We need to take the Gulfstream and land at that military airport north of London," said Matt. "If I have to fly, I don't like that. So let's try hard to get this two military pilots to take care of it. They are right at home in military bases."

"The people at both airports expect military, because of the plane," said Ashley. "We need uniforms. We still have them and can bring the General's."

"If we can use the London City Airport, then it doesn't matter," added Matt. "If we are restricted to the airbase just outside of London, we need uniforms and ID cards. It gets complicated fast."

Matt was thinking and talking fast. He didn't even hear what Ashley said.

"I have an idea," said Ashley. "Tell me if it is stupid."

"Okay, keep going," said Matt. "Remember, your method. The easiest way is the best way."

"We take the General to the safe house," started Ashley. "This is too stupid."

"No, keep going," said Matt. "Out of the mouths of babies off times come gems,"

"That's not too nice," replied Ashley. "You now owe me a dinner at the Green Room, and if you like my idea, you owe me two more dinners. Don't forget."

"As I said, keep going," continued Matt. "While you're talking, I can taste some of this nice looking scone."

"We put a wheelchair in that safe house, the one at Russell Square," said Ashley with a big smile. "The General drives up in his BMW and leaves parking room in front. We have a British military ambulance drive up and the General comes out in the wheelchair in his generals suit with stars and other things all over it. We are there in our uniforms in our military outfits to help him - you're a Colonel and I'm a Major. The three of us get into the ambulance and take him to whatever airport. When a general is in a wheelchair, nobody will question him or us. We get into the Gulfstream, turn on the afterburner, and we are out of there."

"The media, such as the paparazzi, will wait for awhile and then realize they have been duped and go home," said. Matt. "That is a good idea that I think will work. Now I you owe you that two dinners at the Green Room, That's four. It will be an interesting week. Eat your scone while I talk."

"Buzz will reserve the safe house and get an ambulance some how - maybe in the junk yard - and get someone to drive the ambulance," continued Matt. "Then they can leave the ambulance on the side of the road somewhere."

"Maybe Buzz can put on his uniform and be the driver," said Ashley.

"I think he is too important to do something like that," replied Matt. "Being a Knight of the Royal Kingdom, he wouldn't do something like that and by now, that has probably gone to his head. He has a son that he fired in one of those episodes 2 or 3 years ago. That could work. We could give him enough money to make it worthwhile."

"Do you really think that could work?" asked Ashley. "It is pretty simple."

"Maybe that's the beauty of it," said Matt. "The easiest solution is the best one."

"I wonder if the General wants to be extracted," said Ashley. "He could enjoy being the center of attention."

"I've played a lot of golf with him and he doesn't seem to be that way, and another thing is that he is a general and worked hard to get that distinction.," said Matt. "Another thing is that if the paparazzi wants to talk to him, he would probably do it and answer questions. That could be a real headache for the Royalty."

"If he got extracted, the retired Queen would probably be furious with him, and write him off," continued Ashley. "Maybe she would want to come with him to America."

"We better get a ladies uniform for her," said Matt.

"Do you know how?" asked Ashley.

"I don't have a clue," answered Matt. "The General could order it. The military people just obey orders and don't know where the call came from. They are just soldiers. If a general orders them to jump, they jump."

"We could have Buzz interact with him on this," said Ashley. "That gets us off the hook. Why don't you call Buzz, while I go to the loo, I mean the bathroon. I don't want to hear the response. Can you remember it? Don't forget the retired Queen."

"Of course I can remember, anyway I've been writing it down in the notebook you brought," said Matt."

Matt called Buzz who answered on the first ring.

—————

"Did you get him?" asked Ashley as she sat down. "I took as long as I could. People wonder if you are in the loo too long."

"What's this loo stuff, all of a sudden?" asked Matt.

"I thought you would have figured it out by now," said Ashley. "It's like your parking lot conundrum. All I could do in the bathroom was take a bath. I didn't take a bath so I must not have gone to the bath room."

"Then what did you do?" asked Matt.

"I don't know, that's for you to figure out," answered Ashley smiling. "All I know is that I didn't take a bath."

"Okay, I get your point," said Matt. "I'll refrain from the parking lot stuff. Buzz liked the idea. He said he thought the General would for for it, and he could taker care of the details. No problem with that. But hold on to your hat. First, he says that the General really likes the paparazzi. He talks to them with great vigor. He says he has an appointment with the General and the retired Queen to pull a pint at London's favorite pub this afternoon. He says that now, the retired Queen likes the General's antics. He says he has reserved a slot at the military airport and that we should arrange to get the retired pilots that's we usually use. That means that uniforms, IDs, and passports will be necessary. He will get a photo this afternoon of the retired Queen and her requisite sizes. However, the retired Queen is too old for military so she should have a nurses outfit. The sizes will still apply to her. Also, underwear, stockings, shoes, and a nurse's hat. His son will help, and I said the General would pay him and Buzz a million dollars each. That's it. If the General says yes - and Buzz says he will - then he the General would have to order the retired Queen's diver's license, her new passport, and uniform sent to our house. He says plan on two days for the work and expect to travel to London on the third day. That's 3 days after today. Here's what we have to do: arrange for the pilots and the Gulfstream, and probably take care of the nurse's outfit and other supplies. We will fly with our military clothes and be transported under cover to the safe house. We will bring the General's and the retired Queen's clothes with us. Buzz's son will be our mode of transportation from the Gulfstream to the safe house, and from the safe house to the military base to complete the extraction. The General and the retired Queen have to get to the safe house on their own. Buzz will arrange to have his car tailed to protect them. If something pops up, then we will repeat the procedure the next day."

"One more thing," said Matt. "Buzz complements you, Ashley, on your excellent idea for the extraction."

END OF CHAPTER TWO.

CHAPTER 3

The Extraction

The flight of Matt and Ashley from the New Jersey International Airport commenced at 5:30 am, giving them enough time to repeat the extraction, if necessary, but the schedule was tight. It was designed by Buzz and his buddy the General. The Gulfstream landed at the military base just north of London, and they had no trouble passing British security wearing the military uniforms. Buzz's son picked them up in the family's Jaguar and dropped them off at the hotel in Russell Square. It was too late for the extraction on that day, so the pilots slept on the base and Matt and Ashley stayed in the safe house. Matt and Ashley couldn't figure why the extraction wasn't scheduled for that day. Buzz had made sure the the safe house was stocked with food and drink. The flight was executed in beautiful weather and experienced a good tail wind. Buzz was a sharp operator. The minute after the Gulfstream landed and the passengers exited, the British crew started readying it for the return flight. Things seemed to be going well, but both Matt and Ashley were nervous. Ashley thought something unfortunate was going to happen. She said the solution was too simple. Matt just thought that the retired Queen was a weak link, and the General was all the uncertainty the plan could stand.

The plan was to have the General drive his BMW to the Russell safe house and park far enough away for the ambulance to swoop in to pick up the disabled General. The General was scheduled to leave the Palace at 10 am. Drive to the safe house, and have Buzz's son pick them up in front of the safe house at 10:30. The General had 15 minutes to change clothes. Matt made a test run with his uniform to verify that 15 minutes was enough time.

At 10 am the morning of the planned extraction, Matt and Ashley were up early. Cleaned up, ate breakfast, got dressed, and were ready to go. In Buckingham Palace, the General and the retired Queen did essentially the same thing. The General called to have the BMW up by the Royal Car Minder, and the retired Queen said no. She did not want to leave a perfect fully good BMW automobile on the street, as planned, for some idle person to confiscate it. Then the General said, 'We must then summon a Royal Transportation Vehicle.' The retired Queen denied, and said that she did not want to leave the Royal Kingdom. The General went to his quarters, and called Buzz.

"Buzz, this is Les," said the General. "She pulled out of the extraction as we were ready to go."

"I suspected that would be the case, and I am ready to pick you up at the palace gate in 15 minutes, and I will escort you to the safe house.," said Buzz. "Be prepared to leave, and the paparazzi will be there by then. My son will pick you up in the ambulance and transport you, Matt, and Ashley to the military base. You should be wearing your military uniform. You, Matt, and Ashley must be in uniform to go through military customs. You should have no trouble. Now listen Les, I could have told you this would probably happen, because the retired Queen is known for this type of behavior. Just be at the gate in 15 minutes. You will have no trouble getting out. I'm already on the way and am speaking with you from the SUV. When the retired Queen is thwarted in any way, she will cause trouble. At this point, you only option is to just leave the United Kingdom. Go!"

The General hurried done to the main gate, and the guards were cordial.

"Good morning sir," said one of the guards. "Going for for of your usual walk, this morning? The weather is beautiful."

The General walked down the block 50 meters, and Buzz stopped and picked him up. In 15 minutes they stopped in front of the safe house. Luckily, the traffic was light. Buzz shook hands with the General and not a word was exchanged. The General went upstairs to the safe area and knocked at the door. Matt let the General in and immediately knew what had happened. The General put on his uniform with Matt and Ashley's help, and the three headed down the back stairs. Buzz's son was there with the ambulance and they headed to the airport. The Buzz's son let them off at the military travelers entrance and the Gulfstream was waiting, all ready to go. Buzz had taken care of that from the SUV. In 10 minutes, the Gulfstream was airborne and headed to the United States. The extraction was complete and life was back to normal for Matt, Ashley, and the General. The General was more than a little embarrassed. The series of glamorous events were over and the Retired Queen and the General were not legally married, andtheir behavior had been that of traditional royal customs.

"Well, we all learned something," said Matt. "Sometimes, things seem too good to be true. The team has experienced some events that were not customary, and we handled them well. I'm looking forward to a round of golf in our usual golf course, and an enjoyable dinner at the Green Room."

"I'm hungry," said the General. "Do we have any food on the plane?"

"I'll ask the First Officer," said Ashley.

In two minutes, Ashley was back with the news that the staff at the military base had stuffed the kitchenette with an enormous collection of sandwiches. Military guys eat an enormous amount, regardless if you are English or American.

Back in New Jersey, Betty and her new husband, Dr. Richard Hutchinson had stayed in the General's home awaiting his return. Betty had found the General a new housekeeper and her name was Jean. Betty had worked with her before and knew she was reliable and conscientious. Life was back to normal for Matt, Ashley, and the General.

END OF CHAPTER THREE

CHAPTER 4

Another 6 O'Clock Call

—————————— ⚹ ——————————

Matt and Ashley got home, took off their Army clothes, and headed to the family room for a good movie and a hot bowl of popcorn. They both needed a bit of pleasure.

"It's good to be home," said Ashley. "What do you think Matt; do you think our adventuresome days are over?"

"I wouldn't count on it," replied Matt. "It's about time for the government and Director Carter to raise their heads. It's been too quiet."

How right Matt was.

—————————— ⚹ ——————————

Matt and Ashley were both awake at 6 o'clock when the phone rang.

"Ten o'clock golf, wait and see," said Matt as he reached for the phone.

"Ten o'clock for golf, something has come up," said the General.

"You were right," said Ashley. "Say yes and let's get some more sleep."

"Good morning, General," replied Matt. "I'll be there."

"Sorry, I didn't start off right," answered the General. "I just got the call, in the middle of the night. Clark was waiting for my fiasco to be over. He said he knew it would be."

"I'll be there,"answered Matt. "Get some sleep. You must be tired."

—————

"Do you think he had something to do with the so called fiasco?" Asked Ashley.

"Could very well be," replied Matt. "Directors of intelligence work in strange ways."

"Starbucks?" Said Ashley.

"Okay,: said Matt. "I have a unique idea. Let's get some sleep."

"Okay by me." Answered Ashley.

—————

Starbucks was warm and cozy for Matt and Ashley's breakfast, but the weather wasn't. It was overcast and damp. The ground was damp. It must have rained in the night. It was not a good day for golf. During the play, Matt continued with excuses to start the conversation, but the General persisted in avoiding any manner of speech. He was waiting for the ninth hole, where he and Matt usually took time for a conversation.

"Are you going to tell me what's this is all about, or not," said Matt. "It must pretty important for Clark to call you in the middle of the night. He is usually calm and collected. Maybe his wife is missing and he wants us to find her."

"Be serious Matt," replied the General. "This might be serious."

"Then, what is it?" Asked Matt.

"It is AI and he is all worked up about it; and he wants us to bail him out," said the General. "We have to go tomorrow to get the whole story. I said okay for a one o'clock pickup. What is this AI anyway? Sounds like a sickness of some kind."

"Ashley also?" Asked Matt.

"Yes, Ashley too," replied the General. "He said she keeps us focused on the problem."

"We had better get going then," said Matt. "AI stand for Artificial Intelligence."

"He said come the way you are, you don't have to get dressed up, because we are not going to the White House, but to the

Intelligence Headquarters in Langley Virginia," said the General. "This must be important. Let's play faster than usual."

"One more thing," continued the General, "We get to ride I that new high speed plane, whatever it is. It is coming to the local airport."

END OF CHAPTER FOUR

PART II

Getting on Board with a New Project

(CHAPTERS 5 THROUGH 8)

CHAPTER 5

The Electric Plane

Matt, Ashley and the General went to the business terminal and waited. The new plane sat on the runway and waited. The airport was closed to commercial traffic and the passengers waited. Not a word was spoken on the public address system. Finally, Matt took action that amounted to going outside to see what was going on. He came back with a grin on his face.

"Everyone except the three of us is waiting for this fiasco to end," said Matt. "They are waiting for us and we are just sitting like a bunch of lumps."

Matt, Ashley and the General climbed into the plane that was shaped like an old B-1 bomber from the Cold War. The plane started moving and Matt finally caught on to what was happening. It was an electric airplane, named the E-1, that was ready for takeoff, and without the slightest hint of noise, the plane floated into then sky headed for Langley air field at a speed approaching the speed of sound.

On the electric plane, there was no Captain and no First Officer. The aircraft was being flown by a new auto pilot now called Artificial Intelligence.

"Well, I'll be," said Matt.

"I'll be also," retorted Ashley. "We are in the modern world. It's so new that we don't even know what is happening."

When the aircraft got to Langley, the flights paths were busy so the electric plane circled for 5 minutes and then landed. No one that Matt Ashley, and the General could see paid any attention to it. Apparently, if cars could drive themselves, airplanes could fly themselves.

"Where is this artificial intelligence going to end?" Asked the General.

"I would venture to guess that is what we are here to find out," said Matt, who brought a science notebook with quadrille pages, and a couple of papers, all continued in a handsome thin leather case.

The others brought nothing. They were picked up by a large golf-cart type vehicle that drove itself and dropped them off at Director Clark's office. Director Clark, an ex-four star General welcomed Matt, Ashley, and the General and motioned for them to take a seat.

"Welcome Matt, Ashley, and General, I hope that you were suitably impressed with your welcome and that was the idea behind it," said Mark Clark. "That is why you are here, to find out exactly and precisely what is going on in the ever changing world of Artificial Intelligence. We sorely need a report that will serve as learning tool for persons in the Intelligence Directorate. It is a difficult task because there are so many individuals and corporations involved with new AI, as they call it."

"Well, I think we can safely say that you have done that with the electric aircraft and auto pilots," said the General.

"Our job is to find out what our enemy is doing in that area and what we don't want them to do, or even think of doing," said Clark. "Of course we are quite interested in what they even know about Artificial Intelligence just to be sure they do not know anything we don't know. The academic community is wide open, but we want to make sure we are leading the pack. However, we cannot assess knowledge of Artificial Intelligence if we don't have ourselves. "

"Where do we get the information that you so strongly need?" asked Ashley.

"That is precisely what we need you to find out," said Clark. "To be honest, we do not know what we do not know."

"Where do we start?" Asked the General. "Where do we stand in this regard at this precise minute?"

"Again, we don't know," said Clark. "I would say you take a serious look at the literature considering that there is a lot of duplication and copying going on as is normally the case. Everyone knows about those jokers that submit a paper for a conference by simply changing the title of a previous paper. I fully recognize that it is often necessary to repeat things for the benefit of the reader. Albert Einstein must have written hundreds of papers and every word cannot be unique. However, there is a limit to everything. What I'm trying to say, and remember I am not an academic, when is it is okay to copy from yourself."

"There are a lot of papers out there and we do not know that they exist and how to locate them," said Matt. "What I am asking is do we have any resources to assist us in that regard."

"I can offer you two people that you already know," said Clark. "The first is a person that moves around a lot, and her name is Maya Wilson and the second is Kimberly Scott, our super-duper analyst that you have worked with. They are both easy to work with and pleasant looking. They will be on your team. They have been notified accordingly."

Matt looked over at the General and they both smiled. Ashley sat expressionless.

"Any other details?" asked the General.

"You already know the drill," said Clark. "There is no limit to expenses and all of the resources of the United States are at your disposal. Your honorarium is a million dollars per month for each person. It can be increased if necessary. Resources outside of this country are limited to persons such as Sir Charles Bunday and if necessary that son of the Queen named Prince Michael. You are expected to provide a thorough report for the Intelligence Directorate."

"Why is the honorarium so high?" asked the General.

"It's simply on a line in my budget for the year, and it was accepted by the U.S. budget office, so that is my answer," answered Clark. "I would appreciate a report on a monthly basis. It is to be Top Secret, even though the included therein is not secret. That may change but is an open item. Another thing. This may be an easy project for you geniuses."

"There is some paperwork, such as Department of Intelligence ID badges, and how to obtain needed resources," said Clark. "You will be classed as adjuncts of mine with all of the privileges that I have, including the electric plane to your ride back to New Jersey - that is, if you want it. I would be pleased if you would join us for lunch; unfortunately Maya and Kimberly are not available. Kimberly Scott works in Washington, and Maya Wilson in on undisclosed assignment."

END OF CHAPTER FIVE

CHAPTER 6

The Kick-Off Luncheon

The Intelligence room for eating was unnamed and enormous. It had no name. Some called it the cafeteria, others the lunch room, and still others the dining hall. There were no special sections for any purpose, such as executive dining area. In the Intelligence Directorate, everyone was equal./

The Director had selected a table in the center of the room to imply importance, and indeed they were important. The Director's line in the U.S. budget was indeed a good one. A prime filet mignon was served with all of the dressings. Everyone in the room knew something big was going on. No one asked. Things, more importantly everything, were Secret. Everyone at the table knew that was the case.

After the lunch meal, Director Clark signaled Matt, who retrieved a set of 6 papers out of his leather case and handed a copy to the participants at the table.

"It is with the Director's special permission that I have prepared a special paper on Artificial Intelligence for the group," said Matt. "It was originally prepared for the Romeo Club of Sun City by me for presentation at a breakfast meeting. I wrote it. It was presented at that meeting by another person. It is not Top Secret but it is Confidential. Privacy is warranted. It is not technical and we thought it was a good way to initiate a complicated operation. Our reports to the Intelligence Directorate will be Top Secret. Accordingly, here is a copy of that introductory paper. At the time, neither Kimberly nor I knew the extent of the current Artificial Intelligence project. Had we known that, descriptions would probably be shorter. We just did the best we could under the circumstances."

"I must say this is a lot of material to absorb by simply reading," said the General. "Can you summarize it for us."

"You bet," answered Matt. "We figured someone would ask for that. The best way is probably to think of Artificial Intelligence as a process of emulating human thought, since that is the only form of thinking that we know. Let's call it AI. There is a lot of activity and new terms are popping up every day. Some of them are technical and some of the others are used for marketing the various products. We just thought it was best to get that overview out to set a foundation for the advanced subject matter that we will no doubt encounter. Well, here goes with my summary. The actual report follows,"

"The question, "Can a machine think?" is one that has been debated for some time now and the question is no likely to be answered in this project. However, the subject is fruitful when considering "what a computer can do." Here is one good definition:

The ability to act in subtle ways when presented with a class of situations that have not been exhaustively analyzed in advance, but which require rather different combinations of responses if the result in many specific cases is to be acceptable.

Artificial Intelligence is an important subject because it may indicate the direction in which society is moving. Currently, machines are used for two reasons: (1) The job cannot be done by a human being, and (2) The job can be performed more economically by a machine. To this list, another reason must be added: some jobs are simply too dull to bed one by humans, and it is desirable from a social point of view to have such jobs done by machine. This requires a greater number of "intelligent" machines, since people seem to be finding more and more work they consider to be dull and routine.

Here are two items of before I get started:

Artificial general intelligence (AGI) is the intelligence of a machine that could successfully perform any intellectual task that a human being can. It is a primary goal of some AI research and is a common topic in science fiction and future studies. (Author unknown.)

The term singularity is used as the hypothesis that the invention of artificial super intelligence

*(ASI) will abruptly trigger runaway technical
growth, resulting in unfathomable change to human
civilization. (Author unknown)*

It is possible to zoom in on the scope of AI by focusing on
the processes involved. At one extreme, the concentration is on
the practicalities of doing AI programming, with an emphasis
on symbolic programming languages and AI machines. In this
context, AI can be regarded as a new way of doing programming.
It necessarily follows that hardware/software systems with AI
components have the potential for enhanced end-user effectiveness.

It would appear, therefore, that AI is more concerned with
intelligence in general and less involved with human thought in
particular. Thus, it may be contended that humans and computers
are simply two options in the genus of information processing
systems.

There seems to be some value in the ongoing debate over
the intelligence of AI artifacts. The term "artificial" in artificial
intelligence helps us out. One could therefore contend that
intelligence is natural if it is biological and artificial otherwise.
This conclusion skirts the controversy and frees intellectual energy
for more purposeful activity.

Cognitive technology is the set of concepts and techniques
for developing joint human-machine cognitive systems. People
are obviously interested in cognitive systems because they are
goal directed and employ self-knowledge of the environment to

monitor, plan, and modify their actions in the pursuit of their goals. In a logical sense, joint human-machine systems can also be classed as being cognitive because of the availability of computational techniques for automating decisions and exercising operational control over physical processes and organizational activities.

Methods for reasoning in expert and cognitive systems are well defined. Rules and representation effectively solve the problem. There appears to be a set of problems, however, that seem to evade such a simple solution as rules and representation.

A sophisticated model of a cognitive system must incorporate the capability of reasoning about itself or another cognitive system and about the computational facilities that provide the cognition. When a person, for example, is asked to reason about the feelings of the probable response of another person, set of rules is normally invoked to provide the desired response."

"Well, that's it," said Matt. "It is now a complicated world, and we are on the verge of entering it. This should be a very interesting and productive project."

—————

On the way home on the electric airplane, a concrete example of Artificial Intelligence, Ashley asked Matt why he did not tell her about the writing project. Matt responded that the Director said it was "top secret" private since he could not envision how the project origination would turn out. The less people that know about it, the more secure it is. That's all there is to it. It is U.S. government work, and I had no choice except follow government requirements. Ashley understood.

The General was totally absorbed in planning, and was busy writing on the back side of the sheets in the handout. He would never be looking on the other side.

"Where are Kimberly and Maya?" Asked Ashley.

"That is one of our open items," said the General. "I have a feeling that will not be the only open item."

The this point, Matt passed out the intelligence report he brought with him. He had a copy for every person.

—⟶⟿⟵—

The Artificial Intelligence Report

Overview

The question, "Can a machine think?" is one that has been debated for some time now and the question is no likely to be answered in this book. However, the subject is fruitful when considering "what a computer can do."

There are various opinions on the subject. Some say that thinking is an activity that is peculiar to human beings. Accordingly, machines cannot think. Although thought as something unique to humans may have been in the minds of early philosophers when they first considered the subject of thinking and intelligence, this does not really define the activity. Others maintain that a machine is thinking when it is performing activities that normally require thought when performed by human beings. Thus, adding 2+3 must be a form of thinking. To continue, some psychologists have defined intelligence in the following simple way: intelligence is what an intelligence test measures. In light of the preceding section on information systems, all that needs to be done is to feed enough information into an information system and to develop an appropriate query language, and the result is an intelligent machine. This line of reasoning also skirts a clear definition. Perhaps, it is a waste of time to worry about precise definitions, but the fact remains that computers are doing some amazing things - such as playing chess, guiding robots, controlling space vehicles, recognizing patterns, proving theorems, and answering questions - and that these applications require much more than the conventional computer program. Richard Hamming, developer of the prestigious Hamming code for error detection and correction in computers, gives a definition of intelligent behavior that may be useful here:

The ability to act in subtle ways when presented with a class of situations that have not been exhaustively analyzed in advance, but which require rather different combinations of responses if the result in many specific cases is to be acceptable.

Artificial Intelligence is an important subject because it may indicate the direction in which society is moving. Currently, machines are used for two reasons: (1) The job cannot be done by a human being, and (2) The job can be performed more economically by a machine. To this list, another reason must be added: some jobs are simply too dull to bed one by humans, and it is desirable from a social point of view to have such jobs done by machine. This requires a greater number of "intelligent" machines, since people seem to be finding more and more work they consider to be dull and routine.

Here are two items of before we get started with the talk:

Artificial general intelligence (AGI) is the intelligence of a machine that could successfully perform any intellectual task that a human being can. It is a primary goal of some AI research and is a common topic in science fiction and future studies. (Author unknown.)

The term singularity is used as the hypothesis that the invention of artificial super intelligence (ASI) will abruptly trigger runaway technical growth, resulting in unfathomable change to human civilization. (Author unknown)

It is possible to approach Artificial Intelligence from two points of view. Both approaches make use of programs and programming techniques. The first approach is to investigate the general principles of intelligence. The second is to study human thought, in particular.

Those persons engaged in the investigation of the principles of intelligence are normally charged with the development of systems that appear to be intelligent. This activity is commonly regarded as artificial Intelligence, which incorporates both engineering and computer science components.

Those persons engaged in the study of human thought attempt to emulate human mental processes to a lesser or greater degree. This activity can be regarded as a form of "computer simulation," such that the elements of a relevant psychological theory are represented in a computer program. The objective of this approach is to generate psychological theories of human thought. The discipline is generally known as "Cognitive Science."

In reality, the differences between artificial intelligence and cognitive science tend to vary between "not so much" and "quite a lot" - depending upon the complexity of the underlying task. Most applications, as a matter of fact, contain elements from both approaches.

The Scope of AI

It is possible to zoom in on the scope of AI by focusing on the processes involved. At one extreme, the concentration is on the practicalities of doing AI programming, with an emphasis on symbolic programming languages and AI machines. In this context, AI can be regarded as a new way of doing programming. It necessarily follows that hardware/software systems with AI components have the potential for enhanced end-user effectiveness.

At the other extreme, AI could be regarded as the study of intelligent computation. This is a more grandiose and encompassing focus with the objective of building a systematic and encompassing focus with the objective of building a systematic theory of intellectual processes - regardless of if they model human thought or not.

It would appear, therefore, that AI is more concerned with intelligence in general and less involved with human thought in particular. Thus, it may be contended that humans and computers are simply two options in the genus of information processing systems.

The Modern Era of Artificial Intelligence

The modern era of artificial intelligence effectively began with the summer conference at Dartmouth College in Hanover, New Hampshire in 1956. The key participants were Shannon from Bell Labs, Minsky from Harvard (later M.I.T.), McCarthy from Dartmouth (later M.I.T. and Stanford), and Simon from Carnegie Tech (renamed Carnegie Mellon). The key results from the conference were twofold:

- It legitimized the notion of AI and brought together a raft of piecemeal research activities.
- The name "Artificial Intelligence" was coined and the name more thy anything had a profound influence of the future direction of artificial intelligence.

The stars of the conference were Simon, and his associate Allen Newell, who demonstrated the Logic Theorist - the first well-known reasoning program. They preferred the name, "Complex Information Processing," for the new fledging science of the artificial. In the end, Shannon and McCarthy won out with the zippy and provocative name, "artificial intelligence." In all probability, the resulting controversy surrounding the name artificial intelligence served to sustain a certain critical mass of academic interest in the subject - even during periods of sporadic activity and questionable results.

One of the disadvantages of the pioneering AI conference was the simple fact that an elite group of scientists was created that would effectively decide "what AI is and what AI isn't," and how to best achieve it. The end result was that AI became closely aligned with psychology and not with neurophysiology and to a lesser degree with electrical engineering. AI became a software science with the main objective of producing intelligent artifacts. In short, it became a closed group, and this effectively constrained the field for a large degree. In a sense, that is the way the field exists today.

In recent years, the direction of AI research has been altered somewhat by an apparent relationship with brain research and cognitive technology, which is known as the design of joint human-machine cognitive systems. Two obvious fallouts of the new direction are the well-known "Connection Machine," and the computer vision projects at the National Bureau of Standards in their United States. That information is somewhat out of date, but the history gives some insight into what AI is today and where it will be heading.

Early Work on the Concept of Artificial Intelligence

The history of AI essentially goes back to the philosophy of Plato, who wrote that. "All knowledge must be state able in explicit definitions which anyone could apply," thereby eliminating appeals to judgment and intuition. Plato's student Aristotle continued in this noble tradition in the development of the categorical syllogism, which plays an important part in modern logic.

The mathematician Leibnitz attempted to quantify all knowledge and reasoning through an exact algebraic system by which all objects are assigned a unique characteristic number. Using these characteristic numbers, therefore, rules for the combination of problems would be established and controversies could be resolved by calculation.

The underlying philosophical idea was conceptually simple: Reduce the whole of human knowledge into a single formal system. The notion of formal representation has become the basis of AI and cognitive science theories since it involves the reduction of the totality of human experience to a set of basic elements that can be glued together in various ways.

To sum up, the philosophical phenomenologists argue that it impossible to subject pure phenomena - i.e., mental acts which give meaning to the world - to formal analysis. Of course, AI people do not agree. They contend that "there is no ghost in the machine," and this is meant to imply that intelligence is a set of well-defined physical processes.

The discussion is reminiscent of the mind/brain controversy and it appears that the AI perspective is that "the mind is what the brain does." Of course, the phenomenologists would reply that the definition of mind exists beyond the physical neurons; it also incorporates the intangible concepts of what the neurons do.

Accordingly, strong AI is defined in the literature as the case wherein an appropriately programmed computer actually is a "mind." Weak AI, on the other hand, is the emulation of human intelligence, as we know it.

Intelligence and Intelligent Systems

There seems to be some value in the ongoing debate over the intelligence of AI artifacts. The term "artificial" in artificial intelligence helps us out. One could therefore contend that intelligence is natural if it is biological and artificial otherwise. This conclusion skirts the controversy and frees intellectual energy for more purposeful activity.

The abstract notion of intelligence, therefore, is conceptualized, and natural and artificial intelligence serve as specific instances. The subjects of understanding and learning could be treated in a similar manner. The productive tasks of identifying the salient aspects of intelligence, understanding, and learning emerge as the combined goal of AI and cognitive science. For example, the concepts of representation and reasoning, to name only two of many, have been studied productively from both artificial and biological viewpoints. Software products that are currently available can be evaluated in the basis of how well they can support the basic AI technologies,

The key question then becomes: How well do natural and artificial systems, as discussed above, match up to the abstract notion of intelligence.

Cognitive Technology

Cognitive technology is the set of concepts and techniques for developing joint human-machine cognitive systems. People are obviously interested in cognitive systems because they are goal directed and employ self-knowledge of the environment to monitor, plan, and modify their actions in the pursuit of their goals. In a logical sense, joint human-machine systems can also be classed as being cognitive because of the availability of computational techniques for automating decisions and exercising operational control over physical processes and organizational activities.

Recent advances in heuristic techniques coupled with methods of knowledge representation and automated reasoning have made it possible to couple human cognitive systems with artificial cognitive systems. Accordingly, joint systems in this case would necessarily have the following attributes:

- Be problem driven, rather than technology driven.
- Effective models of underlying processes are needed.
- Control of decision-making processes must be shared between human and artificial components.

Clearly, cognitive technology represents a possible (if not probable) paradigm shift whereby the human self-view can and wake in the not-too-distant future.

Virtual Systems and Imagination

Methods for reasoning in expert and cognitive systems are well defined. Rules and representation effectively solve the problem. There appears to be a set of problems, however, that seem to evade such a simple solution as rules and representation.

A sophisticated model of a cognitive system must incorporate the capability of reasoning about itself or another cognitive system and about the computational facilities that provide the cognition. When a person, for example, is asked to reason about the feelings of the probable response of another person, set of rules is normally invoked to provide the desired response. If no rule set exists, then a virtual process is engaged that proceeds somewhat as follows:

- The object process is imagined.
- The neural inputs are "faked" and the brain responds in the usual manner .
- The result is observed exactly as though it had taken place.

Thus, a sort of simulation of a self-model is employed. This type of analysis might be invoked if someone were asked, for example, how they would feel if they had just received the news they had contracted an incurable disease.

The process, described above, is essentially what an operating system does while controlling the execution of a "guest" operating system. Inputs and outputs are interpreted, but machine code is actually executed.

It necessarily follows those executable models, as suggested here, are as much a form of knowledge as are rules and facts.

But, Is It intelligent?

Bandying the issue even further, a sharp borderline between intelligent and non-intelligent behavior, in the abstract sense, probably does not exist. Nevertheless, some essential qualities might be the following:

- To respond to situations very flexibly.
- To take advantage of fortuitous circumstances.
- To make sense out of ambiguous or contradictory messages.
- To recognize the relative importance of different elements of a situation.
- To find similarities between situations despite differences which may separate them.
- To draw distinctions between situations despite similarities which may link them.
- To synthesize new concepts by taking old concepts And putting three together in new ways.
- To come up with ideas that they are novel.

Viewed in this manner, intelligence is a form of computation. Effective intelligence then is a process (perhaps a computer program) and an appropriate machine in which to execute the process.

HARRY KATZAN JR.

Systems Concepts and AI

An interesting viewpoint concerns the evolution of data processing has emerged from the AI business. The task of designing a rule base and an associate fact base is somewhat analogous to designing an information system. Moreover, both kinds of systems appear to evolve in a similar manner. For this analysis, it should be assumed that statements and computational processes (i.e., modules) are the same (or synonymous).

A sensory stimulation is associated with a statement. (Incidentally, this concept is known as associations, wherein a sensation is associated with an idea, and that idea leads to another idea, and so forth. This theory originated with Aristotle and was pursued by Hobbs, Locke, and Mill.). The associations reverberate through the system of statements, whereby a result is finally achieved. The output can be viewed as a prediction. Moreover, the system operates according to some form of internal laws - such as the laws of mathematics.

When a prediction fails, continuing with the statement analogy, we question the validity of the set of statements. Revisions are normally in order. Since a direct correlation is usually possible between the stimuli and peripheral statements, these statements are preserved from revision. Other statements must bear the brunt of change. The other statements, however, can be regarded as the ‹frozen middle›, since they result from internal laws. The end result that a priority judgment. Is necessary: change the peripheral statements of change the frozen middle. The priorities of course

48

are in conflict and the preference commonly goes to the revision that disturbs the system the least.

Effectively, incremental changes are made to the system until a total revision is necessary - i.e., a rewrite of the internal including the Laws, the frozen middle, and the peripheral statements. As a total concept, major revisions serve to simplify a system. It necessarily follows that some attention should be given to systems evolution as a predictive technique.

END OF CHAPTER SIX AND THE ARTIFICIAL INTELLIGENCE SHORT REPORT

CHAPTER 7

The AI Approach

On the drive back from the airport, everyone acted exactly the same. No one said a word. Not a solitary word, like "It's good to be home" or "That luncheon sure was good" or even something like "I'm glad to be out of that government place. It gives me the creeps." No one blew their nose or burped or sneezed or anything. No one complained that Matt was driving too fast,which he was. No one even said they were exhausted, which they undoubtedly were. Finally, Matt broke the ice.

"Did you like the electric plane, Sir?" asked Matt.

"No, I didn't like it," said the General.

"How could you not like it?" asked Ashley, " Everything was perfect. Even the robot that served us coffee with a choice of latte, cappuccino, and so forth, They even had a drink bar where you could have your favorite single malt. You could even have water. You could even have nothing, if you wanted to."

"Did the robot have Diet Coca Cola?" asked the General.

"You don't like Diet Coca Cola," said Matt.

"I know," answered the General. "I just wondered."

"Well, I wonder what we are going to do with this new project we now have," said Matt.

"I know what we can do," said Ashley. "We could contract it out to that Iranian, who could never do anything right. I think his name was Atalus."

"That's a good one," said Matt with a laugh. "He could fix it up so it doesn't work and we don't have a problem. People wouldn't have to worry about artificial intelligence taking over the world."

"Okay, that's enough joking around," replied the General. "We're meeting at the Green Room at 6 o'clock tonight, and we're not leaving until we have a plan or at least have a course of action."

"Do we get to eat first?" asked Ashley. "A person can't think on an empty stomach."

"Yes, but make sure to bring you notebook along with your solution to our problem," said the General. "I didn't know I was related to a couple of jokers."

END OF CHAPTER SEVEN

CHAPTER 8

The First AI Meeting

Neither Matt nor Ashley spent an enormous amount of time on the new AI project. They didn't have an AI books and the Internet had already become too specialized. At least for the easy to find stuff. Most of the published literature was just enough to sell something while making sure no secrets were given away. Matt spent most of the time tidying up his extensive collection of math books. Ashley spent most of her time looking through Hollywood fashion magazines and looking at something of interest on the Internet. Finally, they both left for the Green Room with a minimal contribution to the evening's meeting. As Ashley had said, you can't think on an empty stomach. When they got to the Green Room Restaurant, Matt parked right-in-front as usual but the General's car was nowhere to be seen.

"Do you suppose that the General is really parking," commented Matt. "Maybe that monkey business in London with the Royal family has set him straight."

"He was just doing what any man would do under the circumstances, that is, do what he wanted to do," replied Ashley.

The walked inside and there was the General sitting at his favorite table. He had a big grin like he had done something naughty. He had read their minds.

"I took a taxi and you can drive me home, when we are finished," said the General. " Change sparks the imagination."

"That's the first time I've heard that one," said Matt to Ashley. "Perhaps, we had a philosopher in our midst and did not know it. Right General."

"If you say so," said the General. "You are the one with a notebook filled with useful information."

Matt knew he could look forward to a long hard evening.

Matt and Ashley chose a choice selection of filet and a loaded potato, Ashley with red wine and Matt with O'Douls', and the General had a salmon steak with mashed potatoes and bottled water. Matt asked the General if he were ill, and the General said he was sick and tired of whatever he was sick and tired of. As it turned out, the General was on a diet that lasted until he saw the salmon steak, which he exchanged for the filet and baked potato. He never saw the bottled water but settled on the usual single malt scotch over ice. Life was back to normal. At least, that is what Matt hoped.

The nearby couple that seemed always to be in the restaurant didn't seem to be able to take it all in. The nosey lady said, "They look normal, but they aren't talking, and are eating like they haven't anything to eat for a week." Her husband ignored her and said, "I read in the news that there was an American in England who did what he wanted to do and the people loved him. He was so popular that they had to extract him." She replied, "Do you suppose he is the American." The reply was, "I don't think so, this guy over there is too civilized for that."

<hr />

After dinner, the group moved to the meeting room, and the General just sat there with a big smile on his face.

"I see that both of you have your notebooks," said the General. "I didn't have one, but it wouldn't be necessary anyway."

"We could or may decide to hire Atalus, the Iranian that couldn't ever get anything right, and get him to screw up the total AI industry," said Ashley. "He has a good degree from Stanford and no one would question his credentials. That's it. One month's pay and we are finished. Then on to Maui."

Matt started laughing and even the General had to join in. Even Ashley had to laugh at herself. An then, things got very quiet. Matt knew he had to come up with something at that instant, or they were in big trouble.

"We really haven't exactly figured what we are expected to achieve on the subject of Artificial Intelligence," said Matt. "It is something that is very useful to society. We have to determine precisely what it is and how it will be used. The Intelligence

Community can decide to do whatever they please, and our job is to find out what it is. Clearly, we can't go inside of all the AI people's minds and find out what they are thinking, but we can find out what AI is so the government can step in on it of it becomes necessary. It's like a university course; we are requested to educate the Intelligence Community on AI. We have to start at the beginning. The AI community is supposedly thinking, learning, predicting, analyzing, and so forth, just like an ordinary person does. But the AI community has an enormous amount of information to help it do what it does. I know, some people think it is going to take over the world. So what we have to learn about it, not everything, but what we need to know to achieve our goal. So here is what I think, and this probably will change, is to educate the Intelligence Community on the subjects of thinking, relevant philosophy, and a overview what is happening at this point in time."

"Sound good to me," said the General.

"So lets start out by giving them a good overview of thinking, learning, relation to society - like philosophy, and a very thorough run down what is happening in AI today," continued Matt. "I propose that I take thinking, Ashley takes learning because that is what they do in theatre, and you General take a look at what is going on in the world of AI. We will help each other to get up to snuff. Let me first give you an example of a relevant AI type computer application. There is one thing that I think is important. Sometimes, a person makes a computer program to do a specific job like 'to play checkers'. I think that once was

AI, but it probably is not regarded thus today. Here is another good one to think about. In Psychology, there is a technique called *Non-Directive Counseling*. The idea is to get the patient talking and that is supposed to help him or her. For example, the patient says, "every morning when I wake up, I'm afraid' and the counselor says something like, 'is it ever the case when you are afraid'. The counselor uses the patients words. There was program that emulated activity of this type that was called ELIZA and developed at M.I.T., a leading AI university. Students started to believe it and the administration took the program down. It was popular all over the country, so they put it back up again. Believe me, it is a true story. Is that AI? I'll let you decide."

END OF CHAPTER EIGHT

PART III

Getting Started with
Artificial Intelligence

(CHAPTERS 9 THROUGH 12)

CHAPTER 9

Thinking

—m—

"There is not a lot of literature on precisely what thinking is," said Matt. "An academic named John Dewey specialized in it, at least for a while anyway, and wrote the popular book entitled *How We Think* that was translated into several languages. The version that I have is in French and I had to do a quick study of French to read it. At first, the emphasis of thinking was to solve problems and consisted of the scientific method, reflective thinking, and the role of the educator in public life; it consisted of reading, writing, and arithmetic and subsequently the academic subjects of history, mathematics, and chemistry. Dewey's work was organized around some aspect of educational learning, associated with the Laboratory School at the University of Chicago. Dewey defined reflective thought as the active, persistent, and appropriate examination of beliefs of the information that is available. Thoughts are a continuum of several beliefs. Dewey says that the scientific method of behavior involves deferring to make judgment until sufficient data is obtained and testing, or verification, is done. Dewey has developed five steps, relevant to AI, that constitute reflective thought. (1) Development of the uncertainty requiring the reflective thought. (2) Defining the problem to be solved. (3) Collection of data and other factors relevant to the problem. (4) Construction of suitable hypotheses. (5) Development of methods to solve the problem."

"Now, just how long did it take you to come up with the preceding paragraph," said Ashley.

"It took me exactly one pod of coffee," replied Matt. "Would you like a trip to our favorite establishment as a reward for quietly sitting there?"

"I was not just sitting here; I was thinking about how to get information on learning," said Ashley. "But the answer is that I would enjoy Starbucks very much. This project is going to take some time."

Matt and Ashley sat at their favorite table near the window. It was the table they first sat at when they were students. Through the years, it had become a center for serious thought and amusing situations. They had a tough assignment with the AI investigation, and they actually did not know where to begin. Providing information on AI was one thing, but educating the reader with background information was an even bigger problem. In general, they didn't know what they didn't know. If they were to study the art of making computers do what humans are supposed to do like thinking and learning, it was important to provide information on the two subjects.

"Do you know who Alan Turing is?" asked Matt. "I know of him mainly because he was a good mathematician."

"I've heard the name," said Ashley. "I have no earthly idea who he is. Is he the guy that ran the four-minute mile?"

"That was Roger Bannister," replied Matt. "He became a medical doctor."

"One of the leading persons in developing conceptual ideas about intelligent computers was an English scientist name Alan Turing, the mathematician that broke the German cryptographic code that helped the U.S., Great Britain, and other countries - called the Allies - win World War II," continued Matt. " Alan Turing was a forward looking individual and was involved with several academic pursuits. One of the most popular was the *Turing Test* for determining whether a computer and its program were intelligent or not. On the surface, it seems pretty simple minded, but it gave people something to think about; I am supposed to be looking into thinking. He proposed that if a person gave a question to a person and a computer, and could not tell if the written answer was from the computer or a person then we could say that the computer was thinking, that is exhibiting intelligence, that is artificial intelligence. It seems to be a little simple minded, but it makes some sense. Of course, there is no mention of how the computer would do it. That's why we are doing what we should be doing."

"You could just have a big long list of answers, and all. You would have to do is to pick the relevant answer," replied Ashley.

"Somebody mentioned that and it has a name something like a 'a Chinese room answer' or something like that," replied Matt. "I'll look it up."

"Are you finished?" asked Ashley. "I'm getting anxious to start learning how to learn."

—————— ⟶⟶⟶ ——————

Matt spent a couple of hours looking into the subject of thought, and then asked Ashley how she was going to present the concepts she found on learning. Ashley answered that she hadn't gotten that far. Matt went back and sat down on the sofa. Then, he popped up and said, "What do you think of this approach. We are preparing the information for intelligent and educated person, so we do not have to write down every syllable. All we have to do is to present an idea or a concept, and the reader can relate to it just like we do."

"That sounds pretty good," said Ashley. "Would you like to play some golf. You said I was getting pretty good. Do you thing the General would get mad?"

"Maybe," said Matt. "I'm not afraid of him getting mad. He just gets quiet for a week or two. The only problem with that is that you might miss something good."

"Here's what we can do," said Ashley. "You can just swing easy so we can talk when we play. It makes me think of family picnics, when the men have to swing the softball bat left handed and the women swing right handed. If you're left handed to start with, then it is reversed."

"Okay," let's go before something pops up."

So, Matt and Ashley played their first round of golf together.

———〰〰〰———

Matt was in a hurry with the subject of thinking, because he was afraid things would get complicated and time consuming when they got in to the existing AI systems that people were talking about and were in the news. Therefore, as planned, Matt decided to make a list of relevant concepts on thinking that would serve as an aid to someone desiring to learn something about thinking.

1. Every involving thought has to go through the mind, person or computer.
2. Everything we say goes through our heads.
3. Thinking usually involves matters not directly perceived.
4. Thought involves belief in something accepted or believed.
5. Thoughts implied by certain beliefs are the source of additional beliefs.
6. Thoughts caused by events remind a person of related consequences.
7. Curiosities that cause senses are achieved through thinking.
8. Learning is facilitated by thinking.

Why is thinking of concern to the development of AI systems? That is because AI thinking precludes AI behavior.

END OF CHAPTER NINE

CHAPTER 10

Learning

—∾—

"I've been pretty busy trying to get a handle on some intuitive Artificial Intelligence applications," said Matt. "The kind that are commonplace so the reader of our report can get a feel for the subject and not get all tangled in the complexity of the details. It seems like whenever a popular subject pops its head up in the computer field, everyone and his brother has something to say. Then some nice person says, 'That's really good', and the writer goes off as if they are the world's first intelligent person. I noticed you had started writing, so you must have some good ideas and are putting them in writing,"

"The term *learning* in an Artificial Intelligence context is the form of activity that results in purposeful behavior," said Ashley. "In short, the AI software learns what to do to solve a problem in very much the same way it is done in the minds of humans. In AI systems, the AI software and human thinking work together to resolve a specific class of problems."

"In AI, what is learned?," asked Matt. "Is it the method, the solution, or both."

"At this point, it seems like nothing is learned," said Ashley. "Some smart person designs a problem and writes a computer program to solve the problem, and it is called Artificial Intelligence and it supposed to be intelligent. I have to look further."

"That's the problem with this problem, information is scattered all over the place," said Matt. "And who knows what it means. I went to a well-known retail store that sells just about everything including food and computers. I was looking for a cartridge for our printer, and this kid working there says we have computers and artificial intelligence. He really should have said software, but how it he to know what artificial intelligence is unless there is some reliable place where he should go for information. I can see what you are up against. I've finished thinking am looking for some small applications to use as examples."

Ashley continued with learning, but with little enthusiasm. She was learning all right; nothing in the modern world is simple.

Matt took some sympathy with Ashley's situation. Her she was, a drama professor engaged in a complicated domain outside of her academic specialty. They spent some time together with the subject matter and came up with the following summary of the topic of learning, or more properly machine learning.

"Machine intelligence and learning reflects a computer system that exhibits behavior that would be classified as intelligent if performed by a human agent. That computer system would be known as an intelligent agent, and that field of study is termed *artificial intelligence.* Some researchers refer to AI, as it is usually called, as that which hasn't been done yet, even though that term doesn't seem to make sense in today's computer world. That would imply that an intelligent agent should, in fact, perform a certain amount of learning.

Some researchers feel as though AI can be achieved when human intelligence can be described in sufficient detail that a machine can be made to simulate it. One of the early artificial intelligent applications is computer chess, wherein the program emulates a human chess player. Some AI applications can learn how to play a game and win by learning how to operate without human intervention.

In general, AI researchers feel that any problem that can be solved by a human can be developed as an AI application, and the challenger is to have the AI program learn by itself how to play. That is why machine learning is one of the most important concepts in artificial intelligence.

Other disciplines can be related to machine intelligence, such as advanced statistical techniques, which is termed *deep learning*. There are several topics related to machine intelligence and learning:

- Reasoning and problem solving
- Knowledge representation
- Knowledge engineering
- Qualification
- Natural language

- Creativity
- General intelligence

AI is relevant to any task that can demonstrate intelligence. As before, when a term (or technique) reaches mainstream, it is no longer considered artificial intelligence. This is the *AI effect*. Here are some worthy applications: Healthcare, Automotive, Finance, and Video Games . There are three basic questions:

- Is artificial general intelligence possible? Can a machine solve any problem that a human can solve?
- Are intelligent machines dangerous?"

Matt and Ashley were pleased with the result. They recognized the simple fact that their job was not directly educate their audience, but to provide information so they could educate themselves as required.

END OF CHAPTER TEN

CHAPTER 11

The Advisor Model

Matt spent some time on AI examples and concepts with the idea that examples are a good learning tool as in mathematics. He did not have an Artificial Intelligence library of his own, so he had to go to the university library. He looked at a few references and came up with a short scenario on the subject of using AI to serve as an advisor that could be automated. That would be something like an investment advisor or one that would facilitate cooking or eating or something in that general area. It turned out to be a computer system or maybe even a program to give advice in some domain. The entity doing the thinking was the designer of the program and resulting program would be the executor that gave the impression of an advisor. In this case the expert was nothing more than a program called an expert system. Here is the result of a half days work. Ashley was correct in assuming that thing were getting complicated. Matt thought of an interesting concept that he had to work out, In the meantime, the half-days work looked like the following essay.

"An *expert system* is characterized by a database of facts and a logical engine for exploiting the facts in a purposeful manner. The logical engine takes good advantage of the available information so that the output of the system is considerably more than what would ordinarily be implied strictly by the input. The data and the inference programs give the system an air of being an expert.

One of the most illustrative examples of an expert system is the well-known wine advisor. The user enters a brief description of an entrée, such as chicken with cream sauce, and the system yields a small wine selection, such as Chardonnay or Montrachet – depending of course upon the current contents of the wine cellar. Naturally, there is more to the story. The entrée has certain characteristics that are determined by a database search. The characteristics are then used by an inference mechanism during a "run" of the system to generate the attributes of a suitable wine, such as color, taste, and strength (i.e., light, heavy, etc.) In a second database operation, the wine attributes are mapped into a "variety" of wine. Finally, a selection is made from the database that represents the contents of the wine cellar.

Similar advisors have been constructed in the financial community and in the nuclear industry – to name only a few. In an investment advisor, for example, an investor's profile is mapped into a well defined, but much larger, set of investment characteristics using a database operation. Again, an inference mechanism is used; in this case, it generates a portfolio structure that serves as input to a database search operation yielding a set of investment options. A typical portfolio structure might be: 60% equities, 35% bonds, and 5% gold. The output set would be a small selection of instruments in selected currencies.

In the nuclear industry, a collection of physical events occurring in an emergency situation would be translated by an expert system into a set of instructions to an operator. As before, the processing sequence includes an initial database search operation, an inference procedure, and then a final database selection to generate the needed instructions. The examples typify the "advisor model."

The *advisor model* is characterized by the following set of actions occurring in essentially the order given:

- A relatively small set of input values are entered into the system via and end user interaction or as the result of a physical event.
- The input values are expanded into the particulars for a certain problem domain via a database search process.
- The particulars are mapped into a set of descriptors via an inference mechanism that can take the form of a set of if-then rules and a logical engine, a neural network, a pattern matching operation, a mathematical function, or possibly logic program.
- The descriptors are used as key values in a subsequent database search operation to yield the results for that problem.

Clearly, the salient properties of the advisor model are the initial database operation, the inference (or mapping) process, and the final database search. The two database operations are obviously to different structures. Each of these components can be replicated, as required by a particular problem and its problem solver, but the general structure of the model is evident without necessarily going into more detail. In fact, most expert systems operate in precisely this manner, even though the emphasis has conventionally been on the rules and knowledge-based parts of the model.

The advisor model is independent of the mode of representation; this fact is tacitly understood and is inherent in the notion of a model. Representation is dependent upon a specific instantiation of the model. If the cells in a spreadsheet application are the source of information, then the retrieval and inference operations are related to that framework. If the inference processes are implemented as LISP or Prolog programs, then the particulars and descriptors are constrained by the corresponding ad hoc data structures. To sum up, the method of representation is determined by the underlying problem domain and computational framework. This explains to a limited degree why a lot more "advisors" are not floating around in the industrial, academic, and governmental communities. The ultimate objective is clear: to make the benefits of the advisor model available in a general-purpose format.

Another consideration that complicates the picture is the existence of uncertainty in most areas dealings with human affairs. Uncertainty has been the Achilles heel of the artificial intelligence community, since a practical system for problem solving should take the uncertainty of information or the uncertainty of the reasoning process into consideration. Naturally, we would like to have the mechanisms in place for dealing effectively with both forms of uncertainty, even though all of the features may not be needed for a particular problem situation. It is indeed one thing to map an entrée of beef into a wine descriptor in a deterministic sense, such as:

beef -> strong red meat -> dry heavy red wine -> ...

and quite another to introduce the notion of uncertainty, as in:

small lump -> (((healthy, tests))),0.6),((healthy, tests, sick),0.4))

->... -> ((home, office).0.56)

The notation in the latter example is intended to demonstrate that a *small lump* is mapped into the conditions of *healthy* or *tests* with a certainty of 0.6 and into the conditions of *healthy* or *tests* or *sick* with a certainty factor of 0.4. Total comprehension here is not expected, but is given to indicate that there are different ways to use AI.

In the wine and medical examples, there is relatively little complication in the advisory process, and gives us the opportunity of focusing on the initial database operation. The process represents a translation between the external world of the end user to the internal world of the automated problem solver In the wine advisor, for example, the indicator of beef is mapped into a set of attributes with which AI model can work, as in:

beef -> strong red meat

or in its generic form:

indicator -> meaning

The notion of an indicator is well-established in organized society in the form of symbols, variables,, synonyms, and abbreviations. It is commonplace to have an indicator, such as *successful,* that is associated with a substantial set of characteristics, such as *aggressive, confident, intelligent, and focused.* Indicators can have different meanings to different people' however, which preserves the role of the expert. In the absence of uncertainly, and indicator has a definite meaning. In the presence of uncertainty, an indicator *might* mean something, and the degree to which an expert believes the assertion is known as its certainty value, or as its the certainty factor, as it is sometimes called. Thus, the indicator in the presence of uncertainty is a clue to the validity of an assertion; it becomes evidence when combined with its meaning and a certainty value, or in its generic form:

Evidence: *indicator -> meaning with certainly value.*

An obvious consideration applies to the notion of evidence. As in common everyday usage, a fact "is entered as evidence" only when it is relevant to the case under consideration. An analogous caveat applies to the methods contained here, and a means is presented for constraining the relevancy of information."

Matt came back from the university and looked for Ashley. She was in her office. Actually it was a spare bedroom turned in to an study.

"Are you okay," asked Matt. "You look tired or bored. Actually both."

"I did all right; I got the names and a short description of some current examples that are in the news. If you would like my opinion on the subject. Here it is. It is so hard using some of these systems, that any benefit derived from them is hardly worth the trouble. Companies must be spending a fortune on them. To me, it seems like a bunch of kids and sandbox. Every AI project is a sandbox in which the designers are just playing around in. They are just professors and it is a way to get a paper or a book out of it. If they get tired, then the project dies, and some business or the government that spent a lot of money on them is out in the cold."

"It does seem that way," said Matt. "It turns out to be good for faculty and students and that is where it ends. The ideas are good though."

"Why don't you come up with some AI system that will set the world on fire," said Ashley. "I'm just blabbing. Oh, I forgot. Both Kimberly and Maya called. They wanted to talk to you."

"You don't like them," replied Matt.

"Not particularly," said Ashley. "I like what they can do, if they do something. But to me, they just benefit from other peoples work."

"They might come up with something on the subject of AI," answered Matt.

"Maybe," said Ashley, "But I doubt it.'

"I had a thought coming home," said Matt. "Remember that TV show Jeopardy! Where there was an IBM program named Watson who played against the human experts and the computer won. Apparently, Watson can do a lot of things of an intelligent nature. Maybe you could look into that. That could be really interesting. It could be that IBM is doing exactly that while we speak."

"We could get Watson to do our job," said Ashley.

"Would you like to go to the Green Room?" asked Matt. "We have to ask the General if he wants to go."

"That would be okay," said Ashley. "He does seem to be good at getting things done. I suppose that is what generals do, besides play golf. I'm sorry. That was a smarty pants remark. I'm just human after all."

END OF CHAPTER ELEVEN

CHAPTER 12

The General Changes Things

Matt and Ashley drove to the Green Room and parked in the parking lot next to the General's car. Apparently, Matt, Ashley, and the General were in a serious mood. The General Chose a good table and the dining area was practically empty.

"Why is the place so empty?" asked Matt.

"The President is addressing the nation tonight, and the people must be interested," said the General. "He has a tough job and deserves to tell the people how hard he works. On then other hand, most people work hard and no one even knows it. I guess that is why then is so much interest in Artificial Intelligence to take the load off. There might be something to it."

"Isn't that exactly what you said Ashley," said Matt. "There might be something to it. Just think of all those accountants and office admins that were in the same position with the advent of computers."

Ashley thought, 'That Matt sure is a fast thinker'. And then she smiled.

"How are you guys coming along with AI?" asked the General. "This is a new area for us."

"Here is my thought," said Matt. "So if it is not so great, it's my fault. However, I think it has some merit. The subject of Artificial Intelligence is quite a complicated subject and there are a lot of people involved, even at this early date in its history. It is impossible for us to cover everything. So, I thought it might be an good idea to give them the basic knowledge on subjects, such as thinking and learning and a few examples so they could read and understand the AI literature in their area of work. It seems as though that for every type of problem, there is a special piece of software. Using the word piece isn't exactly accurate, and some of the applications are quite complicated and expensive to develop. What we, I mean they, need is some kind of general package that does everything. The Watson system at IBM is a good example. Maybe not everything but a lot of things in a general class of problems. Now it's me talking again. Some people are worried that AI is going to take over the world and will make all decisions until they get to that point. At that point the AI program controls everything and humans are second nature to the AI software. They call that the *Singularity*. Even people like hairdressers are asking when is AI going to take over the world. Maybe they will give the outcome of a football game without playing the game. Maybe we won't even need people; we will rely on robots. The people will grow extinct."

"That's the best dooms day scenario that I've ever heard," said the General. " I think your should write a book and get a copyright."

"Maybe the AI system will be able to write a dooms day scenario of its own and need a human to fix it up," said Ashley. "Perhaps we should kill the project and make it a federal law not to do AI."

"We could do without computers, since we have been using them for a short time," said Matt. "It would be really difficult, but it theoretically is possible. If we achieve singularity, would it be possible to go back? I double it, because the AI system would not allow you to do it. That is, to eliminate the AI."

"Well, where should we go from here?" asked the General. "For example, what should I be doing to assist with the project in some way.."

—✳—

"We think that we should work together and review the current published literature to give a realistic picture of what is going on in the AI world.," said Matt. "I some fashion, we - the three of us - should divide the task so it can be completed in a reasonable time."

"I really can't help you very much in that regard," answered the General to Matt's proposal. "Perhaps, we could outsource my end of the project."

"So that is where Kimberly Scott and Maya Wilson come into the picture," replied Ashley. "Was that the plan when the project was conceptualized?"

"I have to admit that it was," said the General.

END OF CHAPTER TWELVE

PART IV

The Team Gets Down to Business

CHAPTER 13

ELIZA and Friends

"I don't know how you feel," said Ashley. "But I think we should show the General something curious, not necessarily sophisticated, that would perk his interest and imagination. If he feels like I do, he is not particularly worked up over this project."

"I have a couple of examples covered previously that might start his imagination," said Matt. "They are the Turing Test and ELIZA, both touched on lightly."

"Sounds good to me," replied Ashley. "It would spark my interest for sure."

"The first is the Turing Test and the second would be more about ELIZA," started Matt. "The Turing Test invented by Alan Turing was a little more complicated than I have presented it earlier."

"Are you going to write it down for the General, or just tell it to him?" asked Ashley.

"Well I'm not sure, because if we write it down, maybe he will hand it over to his two female friends and their work is done, " said Matt. "This is an unusual project. It is supposed be our project, like all of the others, and here is Clark assigning people to it, like he doesn't trust us or he, the top dog in Intelligence, is over his head. Maybe his wife Ann is feeding things to him that are outside of his sandbox."

"Maybe, he doesn't know what sandbox he is in." Said Ashley with a coy smile.

"Maybe all of these AI people are feeding the government types with their sandboxes by people from the AI sandbox, which, seems to be a little flakey at the moment, and they are talking about ideas and not actual capability," replied Matt. "Remember, this is at least the third time that AI was going to take over the world. What happened to the other two times? These jokers are talking about things that could happen, and no one is listening to people who say it won't happen."

"Everyone has their sandbox, " said Ashley. "I work in a drama sandbox and it is closer to the interconnection of the assemblage of the military and government and budgeting sandboxes."

"I think the two us us, working together, can handle this situation, as I have always thought that you and I could solve any problem with our diverse backgrounds. Anyway, here is what I have written down. It is pretty innocent and the General could or should make good use of it. This is what I will communicate to him. There is a little more in the written version. It is presented like a conversation. There is a reference at the end; I'm giving to make sure he or they don't thing the concepts are made up by me."

"Alan Turing is an English mathematician whose work on cryptography was a major contribution to the victory in World War II. Almost single handedly, he developed a machine that could solve the German's cryptographic enigma code that was used to win the war for the allies. He is also very well known for the development of basic concepts in mathematics and computation. Alan Turing received his PhD from Princeton University.

Dr. Turing is best known for a variety of intellectual concepts, but the most well known is the Turing Test for artificial intelligence. The fundamental idea is based on the idea that a computer exhibits intelligence when it can answer questions, and a person can or cannot tell that it is a computer answering the questions. The basic result is that if a computer is mistaken for a human more than 30% of time during a set of keyboard interactions, then it is exhibiting intelligence. The test works as follows. There are three computers connected together and two people and one supposedly intelligent program. One person asks the questions and the other two computers answer the question. If the program can answer the questions and it is undetectable that is a the computer, then that program exhibits intelligence. Turing also gives conditions for conducting the "Turing test," but that is the basic idea behind the test."

"There is another AI-type program named ELIZA developed by Joseph Weizenbaum at MIT in 1966. The on-line program uses the input to determine the response, as in non-directive counseling in Psychology. ELIZA is on-line and here is no secret about how it operates. Yet, so many people begin to believe it, that many universities - including MIT - had to take it offline.

The user person just says things to ELIZA and ELIZA responds just like an ordinary person would, using the information in the person's input. The ELIZA program is not that simple. It has to stay on the beam, so to speak. Most people don't think of that when they think of Artificial Intelligence, but it would seem to have intelligence.

There is a Experimental Scientist from Hungary that has looked into the subject of conversational programs and has written a book on the subject. I'll give the reference later. The program, ELIZA, contains a collection of patterns and and a collection of answers corresponding to the patterns. There is another program, like DOCTOR. There is a third system named PARRY. It is interesting when they put DOCTOR and PARRY together. The PARRY program also is known to deceive practicing psychiatrists.

The reference is: Mérö, László, *Ways of Thinking: The Limits of Rational Thought and Artificial Intelligence,* New Jersey: World Scientific Publishing Co., 1990. There is a movie on Alan Turing titled *The Imitation Game.*

"Your presentation sounds and looks impressive," said Ashley. "It should also give Kimberly and Maya an idea of the direction in which we are going with this project, and if they think it is a competition of some sorts, then they have lost before it is started."

"Well, I have to say that you are a competitive person, and I'm glad I am on your side," said Matt. "But maybe, just maybe,

Kimberly and Maya are in the same position that we are in, and that is the hidden strategy. Play one side against the other."

"And the General is the moderator," continued Ashley. "It could be that Clark and the General are together in their own little sandbox."

"Let's let the General decide where we should get together.," said Matt. "That could give us some insight into what in the devil is going on. I'll call him, unless you think maybe you should."

"I should call," replied Ashley. "If you call, he will try to figure out what you want to do. If I call, he will just barrel around me and say exactly what he wants to do."

"Good thinking," answered Matt. "Here's my satellite phone. We should get you one right away. You can't work without one and communicate with our partners."

Ashley called the General who immediately decided that his private office in his home where the meeting should be at soon as possible. They decided at 4 o'clock "He wants to control the situation," said Matt. "We are a good team. Now we have some insight into what is going on."

END OF CHAPTER THIRTEEN

CHAPTER 14

Looking at the State of Affairs

Matt and Ashley were quiet on the short drive to the General's home. Matt was pensive but not nervous. Ashley was unusually nervous.

"Did you bring something to give to the General or are you going to give it to him later," asked Ashley. "Never mind, I know the answer already. It's in you folio and you will make a decision on the fly, depending on how the session goes."

"You're right," replied Matt. "Don't be nervous. Everything will work out. The worst case is that we have to do the entire project alone. The next case is our so-called helpers will do a poor job and we will have to redo whatever they didn't do correctly. The last case is that we will work together and everything will work out just fine. I predict the last one."

"They pulled into the roundabout and the General was standing on the portal. He had a big smile. He had been lonesome and was looking forward to having someone to talk to. He had lost his wife and in spite of her foibles, he missed her. The General shook Matt's hand and gave Ashley a good old American hug. On the surface anyhow, things were back to normal. They went up to the General's study/office, what ever you want to call it. Matt had been there, but Ashley hadn't. It was immaculate. The large executive desk was totally clear, except for a red land-line phone and a satellite phone. The General directed Matt and Ashley to a green sofa next to two green leather bound chairs. A vase of flowers was on a hickory coffee table.

"Have a seat," said the General. "Ashley, I have something for you."

The General opened a desk drawer and handed Ashley a brand new a portable satellite phone.

"Did you read my mind?" asked Ashley.

"No." answered the the General. "Matt called when you were otherwise busy."

If there were ever a good start to a new project, this was the best one ever.

———❦———

The General had his new housekeeper serve an exquisite new blend of coffee and coffee rolls she had baked for the meeting at the last minute. The General started right in with Artificial Intelligence. Not a minute wasted. At least that is what some people would say.

"Have you made good progress with Artificial Intelligence?" asked the General.

"Our question is 'have you made any progress', " said Ashley. "We figured you would outsource your share to Kimberly and Maya."

Matt was shocked, pleased, and proud - all at the same time. The General was just going to learn how to work on a team. In the military, generals just go around ordering people. I real life, a person has to learn how to get along with fellow workers and share the work in some fashion.

"Well, to be perfectly honest," replied the General. "I did not do anything. I thought that I could indeed use our other participants. That's what Director Clark advised me to do in the first place. It sounds like a poor excuse but it is in fact the truth. Actually, I did a little, but it probably is not any good."

"Well to be honest Sir, that is precisely we thought would be the case," said Matt. "I think it is wise to move on from here. Ashley and I will summarize what we have accomplished. If you have any information, perhaps only your thoughts, please let us hear them."

"What Ashley and I thought that Artificial Intelligence is a difficult subject, and it could be advantageous to them a short background, not only for information, but to get them thinking about the subject. We though that thinking and learning would be two subjects to start with. Here is a condensed summary of the subjects combined. I also have it printed out for you. First is thinking, then learning."

"There is not a lot of literature on precisely what <u>thinking</u> is." An academic named John Dewey specialized in it, at least for a while anyway, and wrote the popular book entitled How We Think. At first, the emphasis of thinking was to solve problems and consisted of the scientific method, reflective thinking, and the role of the educator in public life; it consisted of reading, writing, and arithmetic and subsequently the academic subjects of history, mathematics, and chemistry. Dewey defined reflective thought as the active, persistent, and appropriate examination of beliefs of the information that is available. Thoughts are a continuum of several beliefs. Dewey says that the scientific method of behavior involves deferring to make judgment until sufficient data is obtained and testing, or verification, is done. Dewey has developed five steps, relevant to AI, that constitute reflective thought. (1) Development of the uncertainty requiring the reflective thought. (2) Defining the problem to be solved. (3) Collection of data and other factors relevant to the problem. (4) Construction of suitable hypotheses. (5) Development of methods to solve the problem."

The term learning in an Artificial Intelligence context is the form of activity that results in purposeful behavior. In short, the AI software learns what to do to solve a problem in very much the same way it is done in the minds of humans. In AI systems, the AI software and human thinking work together to resolve a specific class of problems. In AI, what is learned? Is it the method, solution, or both.

At this point, it seems like nothing is learned. Some smart person designs a problem and writes a computer program to solve the problem, and it is called Artificial Intelligence and it supposed to be intelligent. That's the problem with this problem, information is scattered all over the place and who knows what it means. I went to a well-known retail store that sells just about everything including food and computers. I was looking for a cartridge for our printer, and this kid working there says we have computers and artificial intelligence. He really should have said software, but how was he to know what artificial intelligence is unless there is some reliable place where he should go for information. You can see what you are up against. We are finished with thinking and are looking for some small applications to use as examples.

"That really seems to be a good to start with AI - if you don't mind me using the short version - and it puts the reader right on the beam," said the General. "Any good examples?"

"We delineated two areas as typical AI applications: Conversational programs, such as ELIZA, and the advisor model," said Matt. "We think we are in a good position to continue with the project. Now General, you alluded to the fact that you had done something on AI. You said that it is not that much, but that is not your style. You never ever do things half way."

"Let's have a short break, and I'll have some fresh coffee delivered," replied the General.

END OF CHAPTER FOURTEEN

CHAPTER 15

A Quick Look at ChatGPT

"I did do a little, but I am not comfortable writing, like you, Matt and Ashley, and I mostly made notes, as if I were giving a speech on the subject," said the General. "It is a general system or a system and product that is getting a lot of attention. So, I looked it up and the first thing I read was that it is called a form of *Generative AI*, like everyone reading about it knows what Generative AI is. I actually have a piece of scrap paper with a list all of those new made-up names on it. At least the ones I ran across. In a system of this type, the seem to be three entities: a foundation of information in various forms, an application model that accesses the data, that can be any form imaginable, and a sophisticated front that generates the information in the form the user requests it. All three entities are complicated. In my mind, it is a system that generates information for the end user. It is analogous to the big computer, years ago called a mainframe, that initially performed a task for the end user."

"Is the subject called generative AI similar to what we call a computer and a sophisticated application?" asked Ashley.

"Well in my mind, it is," answered the General. "We may uncover that it is something else. At least, that is what I think."

"So, the entity named ChatGPT is a form of generative AI," said Matt.

"That 's what I think," said the General. "We may find out that it is something else that is similar. Anyway, here are the notes I took down:

Chat GPT stands for Generative Transform.

Chat GPT is analogous to the results produced on customer service websites - ask questions and get answers.

ChatGPT is an AI program called a chatbot that employs natural language processing to create a humanlike conversational dialogue.

The language model responds to questions and can create various forms of written context, such as articles, messages, emails, computer programs, and media posts. Maybe even artwork.

The natural language processing includes machine translation, information retrieval, sentence analysis, and information extraction.

ChatGPT is a kind of generative AI that involves entering prompts and receiving humanlike images, test, or video.

ChatGPT is similar it automated results and services that are found on customer service websites: ask questions and receive clarification.

Chat GPT is trained with reinforcement learning through human feedback and reward systems that analyze and rank the responses. This is machine learning.

ChatGPT is a product of ca company named OpenAI.

ChatGPT uses algorithms to find patterns within data sequences.

ChatGPT uses deep learning to produce text with the use of neural networks.

ChatPT produces text, next word, sentences, or paragraphs based on some learning formulation.

Human trainers provide conversations to test and rank results.

ChartGPT has been used to code computer programs, compose music, writ emails, summarize articles, write social memos, make titles, solve math problems s, create articles, reword existing content, make product descriptions, play games, do job searches, and ask questions like in ELIZA.

ChatGPT has limitations does have limitations, such as the complexity of human language, use up to date data, poor on analytics, doesn't get the subtleties of modern language, and has trouble focusing on what data is relevant to a problem.

ChatGPT has some ethics problems such as privacy, security,,cheating in education, and cheating at work.

ChatGPT has problems of plagiarism, bias, fireplaces human jibs, and cost.

"And that is all that I have," said the General. "Since Anna died, I have to admit that I haven't been my usual self, but I am slowly eating back to normal."

"General, your contribution has been enormous," said Matt. "We should be able to proceed unhampered from now on. Can I invite us to a dinner at the Green Room at my expense?"

END OF CHAPTER FIFTEEN

CHAPTER 16

Getting Started with Modern Artificial Intelligence

Matt called ahead to the Green Room and asked for a table that would be good for eating and talking. The Maitre d' answered in a strange manner, and Matt asked if everything was okay. The Maitre d' replied that things were okay, but a couple of official looking men had been in earlier today and asked if the General's people had been in lately, and when I said that you hadn't, one of them, the one that wasn't nice, asked what you had been doing. The Maitre d' said your business was not his concern and he paid no more attention than normal about your comings and goings. Then the guy that wasn't nice just stared at me like I was lying. Then the Maitre d' said that he would give them a table if they wanted one but indicated that he was quite busy at the moment. Then the one that wasn't nice went to the bathroom and they left. So then the Maitre d' said he looked in the toilette to see he left a camera or recorder. He didn't see anything. He said he even looked inside the water tanks on the toilets. Matt relayed the incident to the General, who said he would take care of it, and went upstairs to his study.

"I made a satellite call to Director Clark and he had to be fetched out of a security council meeting," said the General. "As

I called on the satellite phone, someone thought it must be very important. Clark thanked me for getting him out of the meeting. I told him about what had happened and said to hold on. He called someone and came back with the following explanation. He thought it was Kimberly or Maya, or both, and called Maya because she always tried to act like a big shot. She said that we hadn't called either her or Kimberly and felt some action was in order. So she sent the secret service out to the Green Room. When he told her that I owned the place, she did not know what to say. She is now off the program for good. He also apologized for the organization of the project. He had a Deputy Director do it and that person was overly cautious since it was his or her first assignment."

"Well, I'll be," said Matt. "I think Maya is too aggressive for our kind of work, and I think we are better off without her."

"I could have told you that," replied Ashley, "but nobody asked me."

"Let's get going," said the General. "Things always happen for the best, and that issue is now behind us."

—⁓〰⁓—

"Do you think the General has finished grieving over Anna's death and we are all back to normal?" asked Ashley on the way to the Green Room. "He wanted to drive himself, and I thought that was strange."

"No, I don't think he is finished," answered Matt. "If you ask me, he was too efficient and organized on his work on that ChapGPT subject. That is not his style. I think it, the grieving you mentioned, goes up and down like a sine curve. His normal behavior pattern has been interrupted. He's okay though and seems to be a bit more creative than normal. When he starts talking about golf again, then I think he is back to normal,"

"How was he after first wife died?" Asked Ashley.

"I don't remember; maybe I was too young and not dealing with him," answered Matt. "We're here. What do you think, front door or parking lot."

"Front door, and let's see what the General does," replied Ashley.

"You are a little devil," laughed Matt. "Here he comes; front door. You guessed it."

—⁓〰⁓—

The dinner. was quite enjoyable. They all ate the usual, except Matt, who changed his mind at the last minute and had a prime filet, loaded potato, and bottle water from Italy.

The conversation seemed to be quite enjoyable, and the usual couple was there, as always, to view what was going on, The woman said, "There is only three of them, but they seem to be having a good time, especially the older gentleman who is more cheerful than usual." The lady's companion just smiled and said. "Even rich people have a good time, now and then."

Matt, Ashley, and the General retired to the conference room, and the lady's friend continued, "Now, I they are going to find out what they are cheerful about."

Matt started of the conversation, "I think it is time to try to get a handle on just what Artificial Intelligence is all about. Then we can make a plan, however simple, on how to find out what AI is all about. If we list every name that we hear, then this project will last forever. If some junior programmer comes up with an idea, it gets into the company plan. I propose we call Kimberly and ask her to query her super computer and come of with 3 or 4 major topics or concepts that might come to fruition. Do you want be to call from here?"

"Sure, why now," answered the General. "No one can hear us in here."

Matt called Kimberly, who answered on the first ring.

"HI Matt, I am happy to hear your voice. I was wondering if we were still working together on the AI project. I haven't even heard from Maya. How's the General?"

"Hi Kimberly, he's right here.," said Matt. " Fit as a fiddle, as are Ashley and myself. We have a question for your super computer. Are you free?"

"I'm always free for you and your team," answered Kimberly.

"We feel that we need a quick look at several important topics in Artificial Intelligence," said Matt. "There are probably a lot of them, since people all over the world are working on AI, and some are even copies with a new name. Also, many of the AI specialists are no more than people who are interested in the subject matter. Maybe only the top four topics."

"I just made a fast query on our new supercomputer," said Kimberly. "Okay, here they are: machine learning, cognitive computing, types of AI, and the Watson system. I think the AI topics includes items like strong AI, weak AI, and so forth. Do you have a printer? Just turn it on and I can find it. This is the modern world of AI - just kidding."

"Do we have a printer?" asked Matt to the General.

"It's over there," said the General. "Just turn it on."

"We have one," said Matt.

"I can see it; the page is on its way," replied Kimberly. "Anything else?"

"Not right now," answered Matt. "I'll let you know. Thanks, we are in a meeting so I can't talk."

"Okay, take care Matt."

"Here we go," said Matt, "Now we have something to look at. This is just a very brief description, and we can go on from here."

Directorate Of Intelligence

***** Confidential *****

Machine Learning

Machine learning is area of study in Artificial Intelligence that is. Usually divided into two categories: Supervisor learning and Unsupervised learning. It is usually considered when designing large scale AI systems. It is normally referred to as an enabler.

Cognitive Computing

Cognitive computing is a technique to develop computers that behave like the human mind through the AI techniques such as expert systems, neural networks, and machine learning. This statement has been tagged for a rewrite.

Types of AI

Types of AI includes most concepts that exist within the AI domain, such as: weak AI, strong AI, deep learning, machine learning, reactive machines, spatial computing, generative AI, facial recognition, chat bots, synthetic data, contrastive learning, and so on. The is a complex section.

Watson System

Watson is an IBM system that provides a conversational AI system that can service in a large variety of disciplines. It typically is integrated into a larger system as services as an interactive assisted designed to handle large databases and other information domains. Practically every element of existing AI technology is provided with Watson.

***** END OF INTELLIGENCE REPORT *****

"That is quite a report," said the General. "It could have been generated with the aid of Watson."

"The report gives us a place to start and a technique for limiting our report, since the information domain of AI has grown to enormous levels."

"Watson reminds me of the subject of IBM computers - large computers," replied the General. "With large computers, you enter requests for information or service, and receive the result in the form of reports or database elements. With Watson, it is analysis in the sense that a user enters requests in a more general format and receives a service of some sort. It is the original IBM model all over again. I think we should be going in this direction with this report."

"I think we have had enough for one day," said Matt. "Let's call it quits for today and meet again tomorrow or some other convenient day or time."

—————ᨑᨑ—————

"Sorry I have asked you to come over so early in the morning and you probably noticed I did not call at 6 o'clock," said the General the next morning. "We all have something to do and I personally would like to get started. You do this academic stuff all the time and you have the rhythm for it. I am not so fortunate and experienced."

"I wouldn't have said it as strongly as you did," replied Matt. "But you have a good point. I also would like to get started. We have to divide up the work. But first, I have to say that we probably should work together on the 'types of AI' category so there are 3 choices. Take your choice."

"I would like to take a stab at IBM Watson," answered the General. "I feel as though I grew up with IBM through ups and downs and can appreciate what they have done with Watson. So if it is agreeable to you two, I'd like to take Watson."

"I took a computer course so I might like cognitive computing," said Ashley. "Especially since I have Matt to fall back on."

"So it looks like I get machine learning," said Matt. "We can do what we want as far as location and office space is concerned, as we have an unlimited budget. I personally don't want to get involved with ancillary problems, and would prefer to work at home and use the university as required - if at all."

"Me too," continued Ashley. "I'm not dying with curiosity with cognitive computing, and would be best at home so I can cry in private - I'm just joking around - well, maybe not."

"Ashley, it's a pleasure having you with us," said the General. "This should be a relatively short project so I would also to work right here at home. However, if we do a good job with this project, we might get another. That is how the government, military, and, in my experience, how business work. So, would we like a brief breakfast at Starbucks to get started."

"Matt," said Ashley, "You have the general trained."

END OF CHAPTER SIXTEEN

PART V

The Final Result

CHAPTER 17

Machine Learning with Types of AI

Matt and Ashley arose early. Ashley had some paperwork at he university, and Mat had the same. Actually, Matt only needed a book he couldn't do without and he was back in 15 minutes and was at work in 16 minutes.

Ashley returned in a couple of hours, and Matt was sitting on the sofa reading a book on projective geometry.

"You are sitting on the sofa with a math book when we have work to do," said Ashley.

"I'm finished," said Matt. "I felt a little anxious so I worked pretty fast. Also, I wanted to read this book, and that is why I had to go the university to get it.."

"Well, if you are finished, then where is it?" questioned Ashley. "You can't just keep it all in your head. You can read your own head, but I doubt anyone else can. At least, I can't."

"It's on the end table right behind you, and I also took the opportunity to do the types of AI," said Matt. "You can read it. Remember, it's intended for beginner's and not you."

Machine Learning with Types of AI

Artificial Intelligence Specifics

It is the study and development of techniques for making machines that people would class as being smart, especially computer systems and programs. It involves the study of human intelligence, but it is not limited to what we would class as human activity. Thus, the subject of Artificial Intelligence defines the concept of intelligence for its own purpose. Like saying a checkers program is intelligent.

At this point in its development, there are no systems that are more intelligent than humans. There are programs that do very complicated things, however, and they are under the control of other computers or human beings.

The goals of Artificial Intelligence are the development of machines - usually computers - that can think and act like human beings and incorporate thinking and acting accordingly.

Theoretically, the scope of Artificial Intelligence ranges from simple programs to systems that are more intelligent than humans. Many people believe that Artificial Intelligent machines will take over the civilized world, and just as many, perhaps more, think that is not true.

Machine Learning

There are two types of Artificial Intelligence: weak AI and strong AI. *Weak AI is* sometimes referred to as *Narrow AI,* since people like fancy names and also *Artificial Narrow Intelligence* (ANI), that are designed to perform specific small tasks. Some ANI systems are exceedingly simple like vacuum cleaners that can roan around the living room, and a little more complicated self-driving cars and IBM's Watson.

Strong AI is a group of AI's, including Artificial General Intelligence (AGI) or Artificial Super Intelligent (ASI) with intelligence equal to humans. It could do anything, such as solve problems and plan for the future. It would have super intelligence. Strong idea is a good idea, to some degree, but doesn't exist today.

This opens the door to deep learning and machine learning. Since the two names are used interchangeably, it is prudent to denote the difference between them. Machine learning is a sub area of Artificial Intelligence, and deep learning is a sub area of machine learning.

The types of learning differ in how the algorithm learns. Non-deep learning uses human experts to analyze data while deep learning does it by itself.

Deep learning employs neural networks and is generally considered mor of what Artificial Intelligence should be. Neural networks is with Quantum Computing as two of the most complicated subject in advance computer technology.

Generative models take raw data and generate useful information. Generative models take raw data and generate useful information. Generate models are not new and are what the subject of statistics is designed to do. The modern Artificial Intelligence method use information to select data for display or other forms of computation.

Artificial Intelligence Applications

Most Artificial Intelligence writers summarize into 5 categories. They are: Speech Recognition, Customer Service, Computer Vision, Recommendation Engines, and Automated Stock Trading. Here is a brief summary of those categories.

Speech: Uses natural language processing to analyze human speech and generate it in a written form.

Customer: Called virtual agents that respond to customer queries, that may be questions, products, and sizes through customer engagement. Referred to as virtual agents or voice assistants.

Vision: Used to derive useful information from digital images and videos. Used in healthcare, law enforcement, or design by computer.

Recommendation: Use past consumption to discover data trends to improve various business goals.

Automated: Used to optimize stock portfolios and facilitate automated stock trading.

"Thanks, Matt," sad Ashley. "You are always amazing."

END OF CHAPTER SEVENTEEN

CHAPTER 18

Cognitive Computing

Several days passed and Ashley was as busy as a beaver. Assuming, of course, that beavers are busy. Her task was to look into what cognitive computer is and to delineate that domain as far as creating AI systems are concerned. There are several ways to describe cognitive computing, and most simple of all is that is is a way of simulating human thought processes with a computer. Using the way that then brain works, using the established methods, and they are called algorithms, for doing data mining, pattern recognition, and natural language processing, the computer is able to execute processes that would appear to be intelligent.

"Hey Matt, I just looked up cognitive computing and a tan into a bunch of terms that I don't understand, such as data mining, pattern recognition, and natural language processing," said Ashley. "Do you what all these thing are?"

"How should I know?" replied Matt. "You have to look them up. It seems as though, that for any simple concept in artificial intelligence, there are at least two ways of describing it and an additional three names for it."

"Gee thanks, I would never thought of that," replied Ashley. "That must be the theorem of name construction, 'For every AI thing, there are at least two names for it,' and the English would have a Royal Name Constructor."

"We better gets going with this project or we will never finish it," said Matt. "Maybe the subjects are in one of those books that have seemed to accumulate around her. The General must have ordered them. Here is what to do: just make a list of all the subjects and we can define them and then combine them into sentences."

"All right, that is a good idea," said Ashley. "I did that when I was reading, Here it is."

The List of Cognitive Subjects

- Conventional computing and cognitive computing
- Machine conversation
- Compute vision
- Computer speaking
- Empathy from computers
- Discovery and understanding of unstructured content (Watson subject)
- Cognitive systems (Watson subject)

"That looks good," said Matt. "You are on your on your way."

"I like working with you," said Ashley."

Ashley became a world wind of activity, interspersed with a trip to Starbucks for a venti macchiato with Matt, and here is what she came up with.

Cognitive Computing

Conventional computing and cognitive computing

Convention computing is, as practically everyone knows, is a pre-planned set of steps to provide a per-planned result. With convention, applications are conceived, designed, programmed or coded, tested, and then put into operation through a person-oriented scenario. The only intelligence is in the mind of the person's involved. The objectives are identified beforehand, and additionally, computing elements are designed to interact of a pre-defined manner.

With cognitive computing, elements are defined and combined to execute in an intelligent manner without human intervention. The computing elements may be defined and prepared or exist in the outside operational environment.

Machine Conversation

Machine conversation is a defined collection of natural language processing and machine learning elements. In its most simple form it is two conversational programs that talk to one another, such as ELIZA and ELIZA or DOCTOR and DOCTOR, mentioned previously in this report. Intelligent machine conversation involves two compatible intelligent entities interactions with one another.

Computer Speaking

The ability to initiate computer speech is a companion to speech recognition. It is usually combined with speech recognition and cognitive computing. A simple example is text reading and speaking. When combined with other cognitive elements, it is in the AI domain.

Empathy from Computers

There are two kinds of computer empathy: human empathy for computer technology and its various difficulties, and the empathy of computers to humans. Computer can sense emotion if defined beforehand. As yet, it has not been considered in the area of Artificial Intelligence.

Cognitive Systems

The discovery and understanding of unstructured information and cognitive sysems is generally combined under the title Generative Models.

A generative model is a deep learning facility that can take raw data, such as database information, speech, visual information, and other event data and draw relevant conclusions.

"That looks good Ashley," said Matt. "The is only one subject remaining and that is the Watson system, designed and used by IBM. Let's see what the General has in this area."

Matt called the General who was in his study reading some information from the Internet.

"Hello. Sir," said Matt. "We are finished with our end of the project and are wondering how you were coming along with the Watson system."

"I received a call from Clark and he said that a contract had been made from a major vendor and the Intelligence Directorate was obligated to proceed in that direction," replied the General. "Everything is top secret, but he gave a idea of the design that we will work with. He said it was a three tiered system consisting of a large user interface component, a back end component that handles the data, and an interface component that connects the user with the data. Each component learns its job through an Artificial Intelligence procedure that learns its job through a classified procedure. It is not Intelligence Directorate classified but vendor classified. He was pleased with the decision. In short the system designs itself. Our personnel will be trained by the vendor and there is no need for the work we have done. I asked for some direction in that regard and he said, 'Just send the report to my office' and gave instructions on how to do it. The contract is cancelled and we will be paid via direct deposit as before. Clark was very cordial, and I think he had a weight lifted from is shoulders. '"

"Actually, I am relieved, as the Artificial Intelligence report was an extremely tedious procedure," said Matt. "Ashley won't be sad either. Does this news warrant a Maui trip or a Green Room dinner."

"We can do whatever you prefer, but I think a dinner would be most appropriate."

The couple that usually just happened to be in the Green Room when Matt,

Ashley, and the General arrived was there as usual. The woman said, "They look more cheerful than usual." Her husband replied, "You never know."

END OF CHAPTER EIGHTEEN

END OF TEXT

REPORT FOLLOWS

Intelligence Directorate

Secret

Artificial Intelligence Final Report

Summary

Overview

The question, "Can a machine think?" is one that has been debated for some time now and the question is no likely to be answered in this book. However, the subject is fruitful when considering "what a computer can do."

There are various opinions on the subject. Some say that thinking is an activity that is peculiar to human beings. Accordingly, machines cannot think. Although thought as something unique to humans may have been in the minds of early philosophers when they first considered the subject of thinking and intelligence, this does not really define the activity. Others maintain that a machine is thinking when it is performing activities that normally require thought when performed by human beings. Thus, adding 2+3 must be a form of thinking. To continue, some psychologists have defined intelligence in the following simple way: intelligence is what an intelligence test measures. In light of the preceding section on information systems, all that needs to be done is to feed enough information into an information system and to develop an appropriate query language, and the result is an intelligent machine. This line of reasoning also skirts a clear definition. Perhaps, it is a waste of time to worry about precise definitions, but the fact remains that computers are doing some amazing things - such as playing chess, guiding robots, controlling space vehicles, recognizing patterns, proving theorems, and answering questions - and that these applications require much more than the conventional computer program. Richard Hamming, developer of the prestigious Hamming code for error detection and correction in computers, gives a definition of intelligent behavior that may be useful here:

> *The ability to act in subtle ways when presented with a class of situations that have not been exhaustively analyzed in advance, but which require rather different combinations of responses if the result in many specific cases is to be acceptable.*

Artificial Intelligence is an important subject because it may indicate the direction in which society is moving. Currently machines are used for two reasons: (1) The job cannot be do by a human being, and (2) The job can be performed economically by a machine. To this list, another reaso be added: some jobs are simply too dull to bed one by and it is desirable from a social point of view to have done by machine. This requires a greater number of machines, since people seem to be finding more a they consider to be dull and routine.

Here are two items of before we get starte

Artificial general intelligence (AGI) is the intelligence of a machine that could successfully perform any intellectual task that a human being can. It is a primary goal of some AI research and is a common topic in science fiction and future studies. (Author unknown.)

The term singularity is used as the hypothesis that the invention of artificial super intelligence (ASI) will abruptly trigger runaway technical growth, resulting in unfathomable change to human civilization. (Author unknown)

It is possible to approach Artificial Intelligence from two points of view. Both approaches make use of programs and programming techniques. The first approach is to investigate the general principles of intelligence. The second is to study human thought, in particular.

Those persons engaged in the investigation of the principles of intelligence are normally charged with the development of systems that appear to be intelligent. This activity is commonly regarded as "artificial intelligence," which incorporates both engineering and computer science components.

Those persons engaged in the study of human thought attempt to emulate human mental processes to a lesser or greater degree. This activity can be regarded as a form of "computer simulation," such that the elements of a relevant psychological theory are represented in a computer program. The objective of this approach is to generate psychological theories of human thought. The discipline is generally known as "Cognitive Science."

In reality, the differences between artificial intelligence and cognitive science tend to vary between "not so much" and "quite a lot" - depending upon the complexity of the underlying task. Most applications, as a matter of fact, contain elements from both approaches.

The Scope of AI

It is possible to zoom in on the scope of AI by focusing on the processes involved. At one extreme, the concentration is on the practicalities of doing AI programming, with an emphasis on symbolic programming languages and AI machines. In this context, AI can be regarded as a new way of doing programming. It necessarily follows that hardware/software systems with AI components have the potential for enhanced end-user effectiveness.

At the other extreme, AI could be regarded as the study of intelligent computation. This is a more grandiose and encompassing focus with the objective of building a systematic and encompassing focus with the objective of building a systematic theory of intellectual processes - regardless of if they model human thought or not.

It would appear, therefore, that AI is more concerned with intelligence in general and less involved with human thought in particular. Thus, it may be contended that humans and computers are simply two options in the genus of information processing systems.

The Modern Era of Artificial Intelligence

The modern era of artificial intelligence effectively began with the summer conference at Dartmouth College in Hanover, New Hampshire in 1956. The key participants were Shannon from Bell Labs, Minsky from Harvard (later M.I.T.), McCarthy from Dartmouth (later M.I.T. and Stanford), and Simon from Carnegie Tech (renamed Carnegie Mellon). The key results from the conference were twofold:

- It legitimized the notion of AI and brought together a raft of piecemeal research activities.
- The name Artificial Intelligence was coined and the name more than anything had a profound influence of the future direction of artificial intelligence.

The stars of the conference were Simon, and his associate Allen Newell, who demonstrated the Logic Theorist - the first well-known reasoning program. They preferred the name, "Complex Information Processing," for the new fledging science of the artificial. In the end, Shannon and McCarthy won out with the zippy and provocative name, "artificial intelligence." In all probability, the resulting controversy surrounding the name artificial intelligence served to sustain a certain critical mass of academic interest in the subject - even during periods of sporadic activity and questionable results.

One of the disadvantages of the pioneering AI conference was the simple fact that an elite group of scientists was created that would effectively decide "what AI is and what AI isn't," and how to best achieve it. The end result was that AI became closely aligned with psychology and not with neurophysiology and to a lesser degree with electrical engineering. AI became a software science with the main objective of producing intelligent artifacts. In short, it became a closed group, and this effectively constrained the field for a large degree. In a sense, that is the way the field exists today.

In recent years, the direction of AI research has been altered somewhat by an apparent relationship with brain research and cognitive technology, which is known as the design of joint human-machine cognitive systems. Two obvious fallouts of the new direction are the well-known "Connection Machine," and the computer vision projects at the National Bureau of Standards in their United States. That information is somewhat out of date, but the history gives some insight into what AI is today and where it will be heading.

Early Work on the Concept of Artificial Intelligence

The history of AI essentially goes back to the philosophy of Plato, who wrote that. "All knowledge must be state able in explicit definitions which anyone could apply," thereby eliminating appeals to judgment and intuition. Plato's student Aristotle continued in this noble tradition in the development of the categorical syllogism, which plays an important part in modern logic.

The mathematician Leibnitz attempted to quantify all knowledge and reasoning through an exact algebraic system by which all objects are assigned a unique characteristic number. Using these characteristic numbers, therefore, rules for the combination of problems would be established and controversies could be resolved by calculation.

The underlying philosophical idea was conceptually simple: Reduce the whole of human knowledge into a single formal system. The notion of formal representation has become the basis of AI and cognitive science theories since it involves the reduction of the totality of human experience to a set of basic elements that can be glued together in various ways.

To sum up, the philosophical phenomenologists argue that it impossible to subject pure phenomena - i.e., mental acts which give meaning to the world - to formal analysis. Of course, AI people do not agree. They contend that "there is no ghost in the machine," and this is meant to imply that intelligence is a set of well-defined physical processes.

The discussion is reminiscent of the mind/brain controversy and it appears that the AI perspective is that "the mind is what the brain does." Of course, the phenomenologists would reply that the definition of mind exists beyond the physical neurons; it also incorporates the intangible concepts of what the neurons do.

Accordingly, strong AI is defined in the literature as the case wherein an appropriately programmed computer actually is a "mind." Weak AI, on the other hand, is the emulation of human intelligence, as we know it.

Intelligence and Intelligent Systems

There seems to be some value in the ongoing debate over the intelligence of AI artifacts. The term "artificial" in artificial intelligence helps us out. One could therefore contend that intelligence is natural if it is biological and artificial otherwise. This conclusion skirts the controversy and frees intellectual energy for more purposeful activity.

The abstract notion of intelligence, therefore, is conceptualized, and natural and artificial intelligence serve as specific instances. The subjects of understanding and learning could be treated in a similar manner. The productive tasks of identifying the salient aspects of intelligence, understanding, and learning emerge as the combined goal of AI and cognitive science. For example, the concepts of representation and reasoning, to name only two of many, have been studied productively from both artificial and biological viewpoints. Software products that are currently available can be evaluated in the basis of how well they can support the basic AI technologies,

The key question then becomes: How well do natural and artificial systems, as discussed above, match up to the abstract notion of intelligence.

Cognitive Technology

Cognitive technology is the set of concepts and techniques for developing joint human-machine cognitive systems. People are obviously interested in cognitive systems because they are goal directed and employ self-knowledge of the environment to monitor, plan, and modify their actions in the pursuit of their goals. In a logical sense, joint human-machine systems can also be classed as being cognitive because of the availability of computational techniques for automating decisions and exercising operational control over physical processes and organizational activities.

Recent advances in heuristic techniques coupled with methods of knowledge representation and automated reasoning have made it possible to couple human cognitive systems with artificial cognitive systems. Accordingly, joint systems in this case would necessarily have the following attributes:

- Be problem driven, rather than technology driven.
- Effective models of underlying processes are needed.
- Control of decision-making processes must be shared between human and artificial components.

Clearly, cognitive technology represents a possible (if not probable) paradigm shift whereby the human self-view can and wake in the not-too-distant future.

Virtual Systems and Imagination

Methods for reasoning in expert and cognitive systems are well defined. Rules and representation effectively solve the problem. There appears to be a set of problems, however, that seem to evade such a simple solution as rules and representation.

A sophisticated model of a cognitive system must incorporate the capability of reasoning about itself or another cognitive system and about the computational facilities that provide the cognition. When a person, for example, is asked to reason about the feelings of the probable response of another person, set of rules is normally invoked to provide the desired response. If no rule set exists, then a virtual process is engaged that proceeds somewhat as follows:

- The object process is imagined.
- The neural inputs are "faked" and the brain responds in the usual manner .
- The result is observed exactly as though it had taken place.

Thus, a sort of simulation of a self-model is employed. This type of analysis might be invoked if someone were asked, for example, how they would feel if they had just received the news they had contracted an incurable disease.

The process, described above, is essentially what an operating system does while controlling the execution of a "guest" operating system. Inputs and outputs are interpreted, but machine code is actually executed.

It necessarily follows those executable models, as suggested here, are as much a form of knowledge as are rules and facts.

Is It intelligent?

Bandying the issue even further, a sharp borderline between intelligent and non-intelligent behavior, in the abstract sense, probably does not exist. Nevertheless, some essential qualities might be the following:

- To respond to situations very flexibly.
- To take advantage of fortuitous circumstances.
- To make sense out of ambiguous or contradictory messages.
- To recognize the relative importance of different elements of a situation.
- To find similarities between situations despite differences which may separate them.
- To draw distinctions between situations despite similarities which may link them.
- To synthesize new concepts by taking old concepts And putting three together in new ways.
- To come up with ideas that they are novel.

Viewed in this manner, intelligence is a form of computation. Effective intelligence then is a process (perhaps a computer program) and an appropriate machine in which to execute the process.

Systems Concepts and AI

An interesting viewpoint concerns the evolution of data processing has emerged from the AI business. The task of designing a rule base and an associate fact base is somewhat analogous to designing an information system. Moreover, both kinds of systems appear to evolve in a similar manner. For this analysis, it should be assumed that statements and computational processes (i.e., modules) are the same (or synonymous).

A sensory stimulation is associated with a statement. (Incidentally, this concept is known as associations, wherein a sensation is associated with an idea, and that idea leads to another idea, and so forth. This theory originated with Aristotle and was pursued by Hobbs, Locke, and Mill.). The associations reverberate through the system of statements, whereby a result is finally achieved. The output can be viewed as a prediction. Moreover, the system operates according to some form of internal laws - such as the laws of mathematics.

When a prediction fails, continuing with the statement analogy, we question the validity of the set of statements. Revisions are normally in order. Since a direct correlation is usually possible between the stimuli and peripheral statements, these statements are preserved from revision. Other statements must bear the brunt of change. The other statements, however, can be regarded as the "frozen middle,' since they result from internal laws. The end result that a priority judgment. Is necessary: change the peripheral statements of change the frozen middle. The priorities of course are in conflict and the preference commonly goes to the revision that disturbs the system the least.

Effectively, incremental changes are made to the system until a total revision is necessary - i.e., a rewrite of the internal including the ruless, the frozen middle, and the peripheral statements. As a total concept, major revisions serve to simplify a system. It necessarily follows that some attention should be given to systems evolution as a predictive technique.

End of Final Report

—————〰〰〰—————

Detailed Information Thinking

"There is not a lot of literature on precisely what <u>thinking</u> is." An academic named John Dewey specialized in it, at least for a while anyway, and wrote the popular book entitled How We Think. At first, the emphasis of thinking was to solve problems and consisted of the scientific method, reflective thinking, and the role of the educator in public life; it consisted of reading, writing, and arithmetic and subsequently the academic subjects of history, mathematics, and chemistry. Dewey defined reflective thought as the active, persistent, and appropriate examination of beliefs of the information that is available. Thoughts are a continuum of several beliefs. Dewey says that the scientific method of behavior involves deferring to make judgment until sufficient data is obtained and testing, or verification, is done. Dewey has developed five steps, relevant to AI, that constitute reflective thought. (1) Development of the uncertainty requiring the reflective thought. (2) Defining the problem to be solved. (3) Collection of data and other factors relevant to the problem. (4) Construction of suitable hypotheses. (5) Development of methods to solve the problem."

The term <u>learning</u> in an Artificial Intelligence context is the form of activity that results in purposeful behavior. In short, the AI software learns what to do to solve a problem in very much the same way it is done in the minds of humans. In AI systems, the AI software and human thinking work together to resolve a specific class of problems. In AI, what is learned? Is it the method, solution, or both.

At this point, it seems like nothing is learned. Some smart person designs a problem and writes a computer program to solve the problem, and it is called Artificial Intelligence and it supposed to be intelligent. That's the problem with this problem, information is scattered all over the place and who knows what it means. I went to a well-known retail store that sells just about everything including food and computers. I was looking for a cartridge for our printer, and this kid working there says we have computers and artificial intelligence. He really should have said software, but how was he to know what artificial intelligence is unless there is some reliable place where he should go for information. You can see what you are up against. We are finished with thinking and are looking for some small applications to use as examples.

ChatGPT

Chat GPT stands for Generative Transform.

Chat GPT is analogous to the results produced on customer service websites - ask questions and get answers.

ChatGPT is an AI program called a chatbot that employs natural language processing to create a humanlike conversational dialogue.

The language model responds to questions and can create various forms of written context, such as articles, messages, emails, computer programs, and media posts. Maybe even artwork.

The natural language processing includes machine translation, information retrieval, sentence analysis, and information extraction.

ChatGPT is a kind of generative AI that involves entering prompts and receiving humanlike images, test, or video.

ChatGPT is similar it automated results and services that are found on customer service websites: ask questions and receive clarification.

Chat GPT is trained with reinforcement learning through human feedback and reward systems that analyze and rank the responses. This is machine learning.

ChatGPT is a product of ca company named OpenAI.

ChatGPT uses algorithms to find patterns within data sequences.

ChatGPT uses deep learning to produce text with the use of neural networks.

ChatPT produces text, next word, sentences, or paragraphs based on some learning formulation.

Machine Learning with Types of AI

Artificial Intelligence Specifics

It is the study and development of techniques for making machines that people would class as being smart, especially computer systems and programs. It involves the study of human intelligence, but it is not limited to what we would class as human activity. Thus, the subject of Artificial Intelligence defines the concept of intelligence for its own purpose. Like saying a checkers program is intelligent.

At this point in its development, there are no systems that are more intelligent than humans. There are programs that do very complicated things, however, and they are under the control of other computers or human beings.

The goals of Artificial Intelligence are the development of machines - usually computers - that can think and act like human beings and incorporate thinking and acting accordingly.

Theoretically, the scope of Artificial Intelligence ranges from simple programs to systems that are more intelligent than humans. Many people believe that Artificial Intelligent machines will take over the civilized world, and just as many, perhaps more, think that is not true.

Machine Learning

There are two types of Artificial Intelligence: weak AI and strong AI. *Weak AI is* sometimes referred to as *Narrow AI,* since people like fancy names and also *Artificial Narrow Intelligence* (ANI), that are designed to perform specific small tasks. Some ANI systems are exceedingly simple like vacuum cleaners that can roan around the living room, and a little more complicated self-driving cars and IBM's Watson.

Strong AI is a group of AI's, including Artificial General Intelligence (AGI) or Artificial Super Intelligent (ASI) with intelligence equal to humans. It could do anything, such as solve problems and plan for the future. It would have super intelligence. Strong idea is a good idea, to some degree, but doesn't exist today.

This opens the door to deep learning and machine learning. Since the two names are used interchangeably, it is prudent to denote the difference between them. Machine learning is a sub area of Artificial Intelligence, and deep learning is a sub area of machine learning.

The types of learning differ in how the algorithm learns. Non-deep learning uses human experts to analyze data while deep learning does it by itself.

Deep learning employs neural networks and is generally considered mor of what Artificial Intelligence should be. Neural networks is with Quantum Computing as two of the most complicated subject in advance computer technology.

Generative models take raw data and generate useful information. Generative models take raw data and generate useful information. Generate models are not new and are what the subject of statistics is designed to do. The modern Artificial Intelligence method use information to select data for display or other forms of computation.

Artificial Intelligence Applications

Most Artificial Intelligence writers summarize into 5 categories. They are: Speech Recognition, Customer Service, Computer Vision, Recommendation Engines, and Automated Stock Trading. Here is a brief summary of those categories.

Speech: Uses natural language processing to analyze human speech and generate it in a written form.

Customer: Called virtual agents that respond to customer queries, that may be questions, products, and sizes through customer engagement. Referred to as virtual agents or voice assistants.

Vision: Used to derive useful information from digital images and videos. Used in healthcare, law enforcement, or design by computer.

Recommendation: Use past consumption to discover data trends to improve various business goals.

Automated: Used to optimize stock portfolios and facilitate automated stock trading.

Cognitive Computing

Conventional computing and cognitive computing

Convention computing is, as practically everyone knows, is a pre-planned set of steps to provide a per-planned result. With convention, applications are conceived, designed, programmed or coded, tested, and then put into operation through a person-oriented scenario. The only intelligence is in the mind of the person's involved. The objectives are identified beforehand, and additionally, computing elements are designed to interact of a pre-defined manner.

With cognitive computing, elements are defined and combined to execute in an intelligent manner without human intervention. The computing elements may be defined and prepared or exist in the outside operational environment.

Machine Conversation

Machine conversation is a defined collection of natural language processing and machine learning elements. In its most simple form it is two conversational programs that talk to one another, such as ELIZA and ELIZA or DOCTOR and DOCTOR, mentioned previously in this report. Intelligent machine conversation involves two compatible intelligent entities interactions with one another.

Computer Speaking

The ability to initiate computer speech is a companion to speech recognition. It is usually combined with speech recognition and cognitive computing. A simple example is text reading and speaking. When combined with other cognitive elements, it is in the AI domain.

Empathy from Computers

There are two kinds of computer empathy: human empathy for computer technology and its various difficulties, and the empathy of computers to humans. Computer can sense emotion if defined beforehand. As yet, it has not been considered in the area of Artificial Intelligence.

Cognitive Systems

The discovery and understanding of unstructured information and cognitive sysems is generally combined under the title Generative Models.

A generative model is a deep learning facility that can take raw data, such as database information, speech, visual information, and other event data and draw relevant conclusions.

End of Detailed Information

END OF REPORT

Index

About This Book

This is a book of fiction and is intended for the entertainment of the reader. The main characters as well as other characters and events are totally made up. The objective of the book is to please the readership, and not intended to give a point of view or other information.

The book alludes to things that aren't necessarily true but are used to help the reader enjoy life, give a feeling of satisfaction, and help that person feel good. It is a work of fiction with all rights and privileges contained therein.

Our daughters, Kathryn and Karen, helped with the book when necessary and provided inspiration.

Thanks for reading the book. The book follows the usual procedure of no violence, no sex, and no bad language. It is accessible to readers of all ages.

The Artificial Intelligence is intersperced with the dialog and summarized as a report at the end of the book. There is a customary copyright notice at the end of the report that may be copied with proper copyright notice.

About the Author

Harry Katzan, Jr. is a professor who has written several books and many papers on computers and service, in addition to some novels. He has been a advisor to the executive board of a major bank and a general consultant on various disciplines. He and his wife have lived in Switzerland where he was a banking consultant and a visiting professor. He is an avid runner and has completed 94 marathons including Boston 13 times and New York 14 times. He holds bachelors, masters, and doctorate degrees.

Books By Harry Katzan, Jr.

Computers and Information Systems

Advanced Programming

APL Programming and Computer Techniques

APL Users Guide

Computer Organization and the System/370

A PL/I Approach to Programming Languages

Introduction to Programming Languages

Operating Systems

Information Technology

Computer Data Security

Introduction to Computer Science

Computer Systems Organization and Programming

Computer Data Management and Database Technology

Systems Design and Documentation

The IBM 5100 Portable Computer

Fortran 77

The Standard Data Encryption Algorithm

Introduction to Distributed Data Processing

Distributed Information Systems

Invitation to Pascal

Invitation to Forth

Microcomputer Graphics and Programming Techniques

Invitation to Ada

Invitation to Ada and Ada Reference Manual

Invitation to Mapper
Operating Systems (2nd Edition)
Local Area Networks
Invitation to MVS (with D. Tharayil)
Introduction to computers and Data Processing
Privacy, Identity, and Cloud Computing

Business and Management

Multinational Computer Systems
Office Automation
Management Support Systems
A Manager's Guide to Productivity, Quality
Circles, and Industrial Robots
Quality Circle Management
Service and Advanced Technology

Basic Research

Managing Uncertainty
Microprogramming Primer

Service Science

A Manager's Guide to Service Science
Foundations of Service Science
Service Science
Introduction to Service
Service Concepts for Management

A Collection of Service Essays
Hospitality and Service

Little Books

The Little Book of Artificial Intelligence
The Little Book of Service Management
The Little Book of Cybersecurity
The Little Book of Cloud Computing
The Little Book of Managing Uncertainty

Novels

The Mysterious Case of the Royal Baby
The Curious Case of the Royal Marriage
The Auspicious Case of the General and the Royal Family
A Case of Espionage
Shelter in Place
The Virus
The Pandemic
Life is Good
The Vaccine
A Tale of Discovery
The Terrorist Plot
An Untimely Situation
The Final Escape
Everything is Good
The Last Adventure

The Romeo Affair
Another Romeo Affair
Understanding

END OF BOOKS BY HARRY KATZAN JR.

Printed in the United States
by Baker & Taylor Publisher Services